SKINNERS

I drew a deep breath and shut my eyes, steeling myself to stoop and pick it up. Only a finger; a dead thing that only the heat of my hand had sparked to a last convulsion. I began to stoop, and as I did so the finger crooked itself again and once more its fingernail dragged it forward. And then again, arching and levering itself on its stump. We watched as it moved away from us, looping like a pink and white caterpillar, scratching the road and scuffling into the rubbish of the gutter.

Have you read?

Point Horror Unleashed

SKINNERS

John Gordon

SCHOLASTIC

for Norman and Joyce

Scholastic Children's Books,
Commonwealth House, 1-19 New Oxford Street,
London WC1A 1NU, UK
a division of Scholastic Ltd
London ~ New York ~ Toronto ~ Sydney ~ Auckland
Mexico City ~ New Delhi ~ Hong Kong

First published in the UK by Scholastic Ltd, 1999

Copyright © John Gordon, 1999

ISBN 0 439 01215 5

Typeset by
Cambrian Typesetters, Frimley, Camberley, Surrey
Printed by Cox and Wyman Ltd, Reading, Berks.

10 9 8 7 6 5 4 3 2 1

1

I should have said nothing. When it happened I really did think the man was dead – especially when I saw what lay on the ground beside him. But by the time I got back to the *Courier* office I had no proof.

At the *Courier* they said: why didn't I run to the office, grab the Speed Graphic and take a shot of the evidence? The old Speed Graphic camera, big as a sandwich box, with glass plates that weighed a ton! What chance did I have? And apart from that, everything that happened was over in a couple of minutes and all the evidence had vanished.

But there was a man on the ground who certainly did seem to be dead, and I'm not a complete beginner when it comes to corpses. Since I began working with Freddie Catchpole at the *Brackenridge Courier* I have seen dead people. The first one was a pilot in a ploughed field, lying neatly in a furrow, right alongside the wrecked plane that had thrown him through the canopy. He looked as if he was asleep, except he was the wrong colour and was too still. And another time there was a man half in and half out of a car in a ditch. He was as paper-coloured as the pilot. And so was the man in the market place.

It was a cold, overcast day in December when it happened, but it was almost cosy to walk through the huddle of stalls on market day. Christmas was coming, and I have a real feeling for the ancient time of the year when it's best that everything is primitive, so I was enjoying the hiss of the Tilley lamps on the stalls and imagining that each patch of light was a little tent of warmth. But then I saw the man die.

It was a bus. It had been slowly skirting the edge of the crowded market ahead of me when it hit him. There was very little sound, no more than a soft thud followed by a wide open silence like a gasp, but even people with their backs to it looked over their shoulders. And he was on the ground at my feet. He had that careless, devilish way of sprawling that seems to say: *It's not my fault I'm like this – it's yours.*

He lay between me and the front wheel of the bus and for a few seconds I was the only one who saw him properly. At first there was no sign of injury, except that his face was as white as marble and no mist of breathing hovered over his open mouth.

From where I stood, the market place rose in a gentle slope to the row of shops and pubs on the other side and I was aware of the crowd thickening towards the accident. But the strange thing was, no one was running. I heard someone say, "Call an ambulance," but apart from that no one wanted anything to do with it. I was nearest, and they left everything to me.

I was aware of all of that in the fraction of time it took me to stoop towards him. And then time clicked and stopped, for at that moment I saw something else. The arm. His coat had spread wide as he fell but his hand was showing. It lay on the road and was half covered by the coat but I could see that it was terribly mangled. Worse than that, it was in the wrong place; too far from his body.

There was no one else close enough to help me except for the bus driver. He had leapt from his cab only to sway and almost collapse. Now he was leaning against the side of the bus, shuddering, unable to do anything. I folded back the man's coat.

It was then that I knew his arm had been severed. It was half hidden but was lying at an impossible angle, ripped from his sleeve and resting across the fat shopping bag he had been carrying. I was taking in the fact that the fingers were still looped into the handle when I was pushed in the back and thrown forward. I had to put both hands against the front of the bus to prevent myself falling on to the body. It was a bizarre position. The crowd was around me and I was spread-eagled against the bus preventing anyone seeing the body beneath me.

"Stand back! Stand back!" I was shouting in a panic, terrified that my head would be forced down to touch the hideous thing below me. My face was within inches of it when the coat was suddenly flicked to cover the arm completely and a voice spoke quietly in my ear. "Leave this to me, please."

I turned my head and was face to face with a girl not much older than myself, but with a complexion so pale and smooth that all expression had drained from it. "I'm a nurse," she said. "I'll see to this."

She had a briefcase and I watched her open it and reach inside for something. She was so deliberate in what she did that I guessed that she could not have seen what lay beneath the coat. "His arm," I said.

"I'll deal with it." She motioned me back, and I edged away but remained half crouched ready to help. I saw her uncover the man's hand and grasp the wrist as if, insanely, she was taking the pulse of the severed arm, but then there was the glint of a knife in her other hand and the thought that she was about to complete the severance of whatever tendons remained made me draw back just as she made the first stroke. It seemed to me to be aimed at his hand rather than higher up and I could have sworn I saw it bite into a knuckle, but then she blocked my view and for several seconds all I could see were her busy shoulders.

The crowd pressed closer and both of us lost our balance. "Keep them back!" Her plea was so urgent that once again I put my hands against the bus and made an arch with my body so that she could do what she had to do. I was looking down into the dead man's face when I saw she was busy with some slender object, no longer than a finger, which she held in the palm of her hand. She was making an incision in whatever it was, and then she peeled it, stripping back its thin covering. And she held it to his lips.

"Doctor!" She spoke close to the waxy face. "Taste this!" Whatever it was she held she thrust into his mouth. "Suck!" she commanded. "It's fresh!"

And the dead face reacted. She had touched a nerve, and a spasm made the man appear to gag on what was in his mouth.

I saw every detail of his face. I had no option but to examine it. He would have been handsome except that his cheeks and neck had been damaged. At first I thought the accident had been responsible, but then I saw that the wounds were old. There were smooth patches in his face, but his cheeks were bloated and seamed as if he had suffered many operations, and whatever colour he had had in life had vanished. The girl was working uselessly on him.

I was listening to her panting with the effort she was making when I saw the lifeless lips make a convulsive movement. And then again. When it happened a third time it was more than a spasm. The lips closed directly on what she was holding. They sucked. And as they did so, the man's eyelids flickered open.

It was then that I pushed back against the crowd with all my force. "He's alive!" I shouted, and gradually they fell back.

She helped him sit up. How could she when he had lost an arm? I stooped to prevent her ... but it was the man himself, the doctor, who helped the nurse to fend me off.

I did not believe what I saw. He was whole. She handed him his hat and he adjusted it with both hands, even pulling down its broad brim so that it shadowed his scarred face. He was not even unsteady on his feet. He wore a scarf, and he pulled it over his mouth while the pale nurse stooped to pick up his shopping bag and her case. I moved to help, but she shook her head. I looked to where the arm had lain. There was no blood. Yet I had seen the arm impossibly twisted.

They began to walk away. My eyes shifted to the bus driver. He had been standing beside his cab, hatless, head bowed, shivering. He must have seen what I saw. But his eyes were on the man, and the man walked. That was all he cared about. He did not glance at the ground as I had done.

The doctor had his arm around the girl, as if she were the one to be protected, and they were moving away.

"Wait for the ambulance." It was a woman's voice. She sounded indignant, as if robbed of a spectacle.

The girl's pale lips moved. "He's all right. There's nothing wrong." But there was no sign of relief in her face. She glanced at the doctor as if she feared his reaction.

"You can't be sure." The bus driver was alongside them, his cheeks still grey, his mouth dry. A miracle had taken place and he wanted it certified. "Let the ambulance people see you."

They walked on.

"But where are you going?"

The doctor, for all his scars, was vigorous. He was pushing onlookers aside. "I'm taking her home. She's my niece." It was as if she had been the injured one.

We watched them go. They walked steadily and even paused briefly to let him brush dust from the back of her coat before they turned into a side street just as the ambulance came wailing into the market square.

"Someone ought to bring them back," said the indignant woman, and suddenly I remembered who I was. I was on the staff of the *Brackenridge Courier*. A part-timer, maybe, filling in a year before university, but a newspaperman nevertheless. I had to write a report, gather details. So I was the one who ran after them.

They were not in the side street and I did not catch up with them until they had entered the churchyard that led to the car park.

"Excuse me, doctor." There were other people passing and he did not seem to be aware of me until I said it again. Even then he did not answer but kept walking, merely turning his head towards me slightly. His mouth was hidden by his scarf, and what I could see of his face was so stiffened by scars it was immobile, and his eyes were as expressionless as a bird's. "The ambulance has arrived," I said.

"Well?" His voice had a phlegmy rumble.

"Wouldn't it be a good idea if…?" I looked towards the girl, his nurse, expecting her to support me. She did not even glance in my direction but walked on, clinging to his arm; the arm I believed had been severed. "I thought," I began, "I mean, everyone thought you had been badly injured… Very badly."

The girl looked at me then, and shook her head.

"But it was the arm," I persisted. "I thought I saw—" But the doctor did not let me finish.

His voice clattered in his throat. "You saw a man slightly concussed and quickly revived."

That was all. I was dismissed, but at last I began to behave like a reporter. "May I have your name, doctor?"

The cold stare of his eyes was his answer.

"I'm from the *Courier*." There was no response, but I persevered. "A lot of people will be interested… Everyone saw what happened."

"Nothing happened." He nodded towards the girl. "As she will confirm."

"Your name?" I was doorstepping; I began to enjoy it. And he reacted.

"Goodwin." That was all. He turned his back on me.

"Could I have your address?"

"Use the phone book."

The door of the reporters' room caught on the lumpy brown lino as it always did. I would have preferred to enter in silence. There was no Doctor Goodwin in the phone book. I had failed to get the story and I was going to keep quiet about it. Maybe I had misheard the name, but anyway the accident could hardly count as news, even for the *Courier*. I had leapt to the conclusion that a man had been mangled and had died – that I had seen him dead. But he had hardly been hurt, so why bother? Nobody would ever know about the arm. The shock of the moment and my fevered imagination had invented it.

Freddie Catchpole, sitting at the chief reporter's desk in the corner, didn't even look up. He was of the old school, like everything else at the *Brackenridge Courier* – candlestick telephones still worked, didn't they, so why bother with computers? Freddie sagged like a tired cushion and breathed smoke into the typewriter at which he was hammering with two fingers. The typewriter was old, the carbon paper had a track record that had punctured it all over, and the bottom layer of the pile in his in-tray had been laid down in the time of the pyramids. But Freddie Catchpole could write beautiful tiny shorthand while he squinted around a cigarette and dribbled ash on his overcoat; he had a personal beer mug hanging behind the bar in at least three pubs in town, and he knew everyone.

"Let's see it, then," he said.

I had no idea what he meant but his tone told me I was in his bad books again. Freddie did not take to newcomers, especially those as young as me, with no experience, and he was certain I was only there because my father knew the editor. He was wrong, but only the sour side ever rang true for Freddie.

"Elderly man knocked down in the market…" Clatter of keys… "You were there…" Two-fingered tattoo; then silence.

I stood dumbly amid the smell of old yellow newspaper and the vinegary reek of printer's ink. I already enjoyed it; Freddie lived on it.

Without looking away from his typewriter he held out a hand, grimed with ink because the chief reporter on the *Courier* also corrected proofs; we did not run to luxuries, or even staff. "Copy." His fingers twitched in my direction. "Where's your copy?"

There was no copy. I hadn't written any.

"Jesus Christ, boy, they're all talking about it! I've heard so much I could bloody well write it myself."

Then why the hell don't you, you screwed up old git? His overcoat was open, his scarf hung loose, and smoke corkscrewed up his nostrils. His little eyes knew what I was thinking. "Christ, boy," he said, and turned away. I wondered if I had hurt his feelings.

"I got the bus driver's name." At least I was certain of that; I'd heard people in the crowd say it. "Tom Woolley."

"Address?" I had to tell him I didn't know, but he was already mumbling as he wrote on a wad of copy paper, "Parker's Lane – little house at the end." So chief reporter Freddie Catchpole had known all along. "Drunk?"

"I haven't even been to the pub." But I was thinking of it.

"Not you, you fool. Tom Woolley."

"I couldn't tell."

"Well if he was drunk, it would have been the first time. He's teetotal."

And Freddie still hadn't finished with me. "Who's the man?"

"He's a doctor," I said. "Doctor Goodwin."

Freddie knew everyone. "Never heard of him."

I told him I'd tried the phone book, and I tried to redeem myself by describing his mangled face.

This was too much for Freddie. "There's no doctor in this town with a face anything like that!"

"Well I saw him!" And once I'd defied him that far, I went further. "And he walked away without a scratch, so where's the story?"

But it was Freddie who decided what was a story and what wasn't. He sent me out to chase it up.

If he hadn't, I would never have found the finger in the gutter.

2

It was dark, and a meagre snow was beginning to dust the ground when I saw the finger. It was a little stick of raw flesh amid the market rubbish in the gutter. I stooped and could make out the small oval of the nail. Then I looked away, hoping that someone was watching and would relieve me of the responsibility of picking it up. No one paid any attention to me – or it.

I moved so that I stood over it to prevent it being trodden on and then, with the strange detachment that a crisis often brings, I looked for signs of blood. Pellets of hard snow swirled along the gutter but none were stained. I checked that this was the place that the doctor had fallen, for there was no doubt in my mind that this must be a finger torn from him by the impact ... and yet it was surely impossible, for he had shown no sign of injury and no blood had been spilled. I gazed down again. It was a human finger, and there could be no doubt it was there because of the accident. It had been so badly mangled that its naked sinews were exposed. I could not understand how someone so badly injured could have walked away without showing any pain.

The dilemma triggered me to stoop suddenly and pick it up. Strangely, it was the dirty cabbage leaf against which it rested and the grime of the gutter that were more repugnant than the finger itself, for it had been cleanly severed so that the knuckle-bone showed white at its base without a hint of rawness or blood. It was necessary to wrap it in something, but that gave me a problem that even at the time I saw was absurd. I held the finger in my right hand, but my handkerchief was in my right-hand trouser pocket and I did not feel I could reach for it with the hand contaminated by contact. I was reaching around with my left hand and looking towards the market stalls, hoping that my contortions would not be noticed, when I saw that I was being watched.

I wished it had not been Hazel Elliott. Loud girls can be a problem, but it's the quiet ones who trouble me. If they are like Hazel Elliott they seem to have a secret that they may be willing to share with you but which you will never quite understand. Those eyes of hers looked at me as I was twisting around, making a fool of myself, and suddenly all my disgust with the severed finger was transferred to her. I wanted to be cruel – tell her that her black skirt was far too short and her shoes too chunky; that she simply couldn't carry it off.

But our eyes had met, and she blushed as shy girls do, and I was about to turn away when I felt that hideous, lopped finger twitch. In that instant Hazel Elliott was far away and forgotten. My eyes were on the finger. It lay in my palm as if it grew there naturally and would curl with my other fingers if I were to clench my fist. I did not have the courage to try. I was grimacing with the strain of preventing myself hurling the repellent thing from me when a voice close to me spoke my name.

"Donald?" Hazel Elliott was worried. "Aren't you feeling well?"

I had no need to speak. I advanced my hand so that she could see what rested there, and the sharp intake of her breath gave me courage. "There was an accident here today," I said. "There was a man…"

I got no further. The warmth of my hand was having an effect on the finger. It slowly bent itself at the knuckle. I felt the fingernail hook my skin and the rub as it pulled itself forward so that the naked bone of its stump tickled my palm.

I could take no more. I rid myself of it, casting it down and rubbing my palm against my coat to scrub away the dreadful feel of it. We stood looking down at it. Nothing would make me pick it up.

But then the anxiety that always seemed to lurk somewhere in Hazel Elliott's face was turned on me and told me what I did not want to know. We could not leave it there. One of us had to do something.

"I'll stay here," I said, meaning I would prevent it being squashed underfoot. "You go and tell the police."

She nodded. I knew what she was thinking. We were both cowards. I drew a deep breath and shut my eyes, steeling myself to stoop and pick it up. Only a finger; a dead thing that only the heat of my hand had sparked to a last convulsion. I began to stoop, and as I did so the finger crooked itself again and once more its fingernail dragged it forward. And then again, arching and levering itself on its stump. We watched as it moved away from us, looping like a pink and white caterpillar, scratching the road and scuffling into the rubbish of the gutter.

Discarded vegetables and leaves from a stall were piled there and it was half hidden before I acted. I scuffed the leaves away with my foot. I would tread on it while Hazel Elliott ran for help. I lost my balance and as I reached for her shoulder to steady myself my eyes caught a glimpse of someone

16

standing at the corner of one of the stalls and taking an intense interest in what was happening. It was a woman, too far away to be recognized in this light, but in that instant Hazel gave a squeal of fright and I think I also shouted because, as I disturbed the rubbish with my foot, a rat skittered over my toe and its teeth closed on the flesh of the finger. It ran, with its meal twisting in its mouth, and we gave chase.

3

It was a hopeless chase. The rat had the advantage of hiding under piles of crates and dodging beneath the slots of duckboards while we had to circle the stalls, barging shoppers and shouting, "There's a rat! Kill it!" Twice we nearly cornered it and when we drove it to the edge of the market we thought we had a chance in the roadway. We spotted it skirting the old stone horse-trough and we charged, splitting up to run around both sides. My eyes were searching the ground and I did not see the woman until I cannoned into her.

"Oops!" she cried. There are many ways of saying the same short syllable. Most women would have sounded affronted, almost as if I had assaulted them, but Beatrice Cole was not in the least offended. She even allowed me to steady her without drawing back. "So it's you," she said. "I might have known."

"I'm afraid so," I admitted. I almost said, "Yes, Miss," for Beatrice Cole had been my English teacher until a few months ago. "Chasing a rat," I said.

"Always in pursuit of something, Donald. But all you caught was me." She glanced down to where my hand was still holding her elbow and she smiled.

Hazel Elliott had circled the trough and stood panting behind her. Miss Cole must have known but she did not turn round. Miss Cole ... she was not old enough to merit the Miss. But how old was she? It was a stupid thought, and the small round face that looked up at me suddenly wrinkled its eyes as if she guessed what I was thinking. She was the same as any other girl who might have been standing there with a few flakes caught in her black hair.

"Where did it go?" Hazel was struggling to get her breath. "Did you see it, Miss?" For her the Miss was appropriate; she had still not put school behind her.

"I saw nothing." Beatrice Cole answered her but did not take her eyes from me. She paused until I became aware I was still holding her elbow. When I stepped back she said, "Surely it's getting too dark to chase anything as small as a rat." The winter afternoon was closing in. "What's so special about it, anyway?"

"Nothing," I said quickly. I wasn't going to tell her about a finger that walked. That was too childish. I had made some sort of mistake.

"But…" That was Hazel Elliott, being honest, a good little girl.

"But—?" Miss Cole encouraged her.

Hazel's eyes were on me, wide and misty grey. She wanted to lie, for my sake, but she didn't know how. She looked at the ground without answering, so Beatrice Cole turned away. "Donald will tell me," she said.

"We thought it had something in its mouth," I began, when Hazel Elliott, backing me up too eagerly, interrupted.

"It looked like a finger," she said, but then saw my face.

"A finger?" Beatrice Cole looked from her to me, and waited.

I shook my head. "No. It was just an association of ideas because there was an accident here earlier today."

"I know." She had not been in the crowd or I would have seen her. The news had quickly got around. "I thought no one was hurt."

I nodded. "What we saw wasn't anything like a finger. It was a chicken leg." There was a butcher's stall nearby. "A bit of offal or something from there."

"Are you sure?" Beatrice Cole cocked her head and looked at me smiling slyly.

"Certain."

"So this episode won't get into your report in the *Courier*."

I laughed. "Can you see the *Courier* doing anything about a phantom finger?"

"But if anything happens you will let me know?"

"If you're interested."

Now she was laughing. "I'm *fascinated*, Donald. It could be your first scoop."

It was the wrong word, and when she left I said so to Hazel Elliott. "It's never called a scoop," I told her. "If you've got to call it anything it's a 'beat' " — even on the *Courier*, so far behind the times that it had never seen a computer. Our proprietor and editor, isolated in his office upstairs, ran it more as a hobby than anything else; his real business was the stationery shop, behind which was the print works with the reporters' room above. "If it wasn't for Freddie's typewriter," I said, "Dickens could walk into that place and expect to find a quill pen and an inkwell."

But Hazel had not been listening. "You don't believe it was a chicken leg," she said.

"I do now." She rattled me. Hadn't she noticed that Beatrice Cole and I were laughing the whole thing off? "That finger was just one of those things from a joke shop," I told her, as the latest and most likely explanation slid into my mind. "You know – horrible masks and rubber claws. There's a stall on the market."

"It moved." She had to say it even though I could see it cost her an effort to contradict me. "We saw it, Donald."

"We thought we did." I had no more time to spend on it, or on Hazel Elliott who was showing signs of wanting too much from me. The false finger had bewildered me only in the aftermath of the accident. It was all in the past. I looked away from her along the aisle between the stalls. There were patches of light and darkness, and suddenly, in the glare of a Tilley lamp, a face was spotlighted. A pale girl, made whiter by the glare, was gazing at us with the same intensity as the female shape I had seen watching us earlier, and I recognized her.

"Got to go," I said. "There's a deadline I've got to meet." I was already running, for the pale girl was the nurse who had stooped over the doctor. Shoppers got in my way, I jinked past them but the delay was too much. She had moved between the stalls and disappeared. In a sense, I was relieved and I did not make much of an effort to follow her. It might have been the wrong girl, and I had made too many mistakes already.

I had lied to Hazel Elliott. There was no deadline, and if anyone was going to play down a story when I got back to the office it was me. But I did have to face Freddie Catchpole and tell him that I had turned up nothing on the accident. And then I made the mistake of saying to him that maybe I could go home as it was getting late. No I bloody couldn't … did I see that pile of wedding forms in the corner? Get them written up.

Only funerals were more tedious than wedding reports. "Journalism!" I said under my breath, but he heard. "OK, Freddie," I said, "I know they're the very stuff that sells the *Courier*." He'd told me often enough.

I got my head down over brides in gowns of white tulle with matching accessories and I thought I'd escaped the whip. But Freddie Catchpole never let anything ride.

"Christmas is coming," he said.

"You're right." I tried to be cheerful. "It'll be good to get away from this for a couple of days." Another mistake. Freddie had made sure I knew from the start that a reporter was never off duty, so I spoke as if I had learnt the lesson. "I mean if nothing happens. There certainly won't be anything to write about where I live, out in the wilderness." Our house is miles outside town where the hills become so steep they are difficult to farm and the forest seems to creep further down the valley every year. "I'm just looking forward to having a couple of days away from the typewriter."

Freddie's head was bent over the reporters' room diary. It lived on his desk for he was the one who marked it, putting the initials of his staff beside the jobs they were to do – not that he had much choice, for there were only two of us besides himself. "I'm putting you down for a special," he said. "It should make a double-page spread, with pics. And you won't have to leave home."

"A special," I repeated. He sometimes called it a "colour piece" which meant that straightforward reporting gave way to writing with some imagination in it. He fancied that he himself was the master of fine writing, but he turned in stuff loaded with more adjectives than flowers on a hearse and it made you wince like a fingernail scratching a blackboard. He was honouring me by giving me my chance.

"You know Oscar Bullimore," he said. I nodded; everyone has heard of Oscar. I happened to have met him, more than once, and I had bragged about it in front of Freddie. "Well you can do me a colour piece on Christmas and bring Mr Bullimore into it."

I gazed at him, not knowing how to object. Oscar Bullimore may be famous enough as a writer for his name to decorate any newspaper article, but there's nothing at all to associate him with Christmas. Freddie mistook the reason for my silence, thinking I was overawed at the prospect of turning in a piece that would match the standards set by his own writing. "You don't have to worry about it," he said. "Just hand in your copy and I'll dress it up a bit to get the atmosphere."

"But Oscar Bullimore is a *horror* writer."

"I know that – he writes about ghosts and that sort of thing."

"You can hardly call him festive." I wanted out of this task. "Our readers wouldn't think that was very cosy or Christmassy." I was working in the yuck factor. "He's not to everyone's taste; think of the kiddies."

But Freddie had an answer. "Everyone likes a bit of horror in the season of goodwill," he said, and my initials went into the book.

4

Chance gave me a helping hand with Freddie's Christmas special. Oscar Bullimore came to stay with us. Not because he'd been asked but because, as he rang up to tell my father, he wished to absent himself from the hurly-burly of London life – he needed a retreat.

"Seeking a retreat, is he?" My mother was not pleased. "Well he can retreat as far as he likes ... and take all his literary friends with him."

She had a point. Oscar Bullimore, whose books are sold all over the world, has brought some weird people to see us over the years.

"Take it easy, Joyce." My father tried to mollify her. "The poor old boy's on his own this time, and he's a bit down in the dumps by the sound of him. Quite pathetic."

She was not buying the pathetic bit; and when Oscar Bullimore arrived it seemed that she was quite right.

"Good of you to take in this old ragamuffin," he wheezed as the taxi gave birth to him at our doorstep. "Worn and torn and badly in need of blessed quietude. Greetings to all." He lifted his tweedy cap an inch and puffed out his moustache as he turned his attention on my father. "But it'll be a bonus for you, Jim – you can have first shufti at the new magnum opus. Got it in me bag."

His slang was as out of date as the way he dressed, and it was all of a piece with the baggy way he wrote, as my father knew better than anyone. He was Oscar's editor at the publisher Keene and Greet, so he was the one who mended the holes in Oscar's plots and tightened his sagging grammar, and yet the name of Jim Price never appeared anywhere when the books were published.

"Devil's own job to find you in the dark tonight," said Oscar as he stood in our hall unwinding the loops of his scarf. "Driver didn't seem to know how to get here."

"That always happens," said my father. "We are a bit out of the way."

"Which is why I chose you, dear boy."

"If you'd given me a ring I could have picked you up at the junction." It was twenty miles away but my father drove there every day to catch a train to the London office.

"Junction?" Oscar's checked overcoat was large enough to look like a cape and he seemed made breathless by the weight of it as he unbuttoned. "I was nowhere near any junction."

"But the taxi," my father pointed out. "You must have got that at the junction."

"Did not." Oscar let me help him off with his coat.

"Had to be," my father insisted. "There's nowhere else."

"Hammersmith," Oscar grunted. "Got a cab near home."

"But that's…" My father broke off; the expense appalled him.

Oscar's glasses, dangling on a black ribbon around his neck, were causing him trouble with his scarf. My mother was watching as I and my father hovered around the great man. "I thought you enjoyed talking to people on trains, Oscar," she said pointedly. Everyone knew that Oscar Bullimore revelled in being recognized.

"Not for the present," he mumbled, not looking at her. "Need to be away from it all."

My father laughed. "It's not like you to run away, Oscar."

At this, the old elephant reacted. His head came up and his voice strengthened. "Run away? I do not *run*, Jim boy. You should know that better than anyone. I have drawn back only in order to make a final *charge*!" He raised his fist and the ring of his voice made the dinner gong hum.

My father grinned. He enjoyed goading the old boy, and he was the only one at Keene and Greet who dared to do it. Every Oscar Bullimore manuscript was more of a rich compost heap than a novel when it landed on Jim Price's desk, and Oscar Bullimore knew where his debt lay. Nevertheless they liked each other and worked well together, but Oscar had never been able to fathom why his famous charm had never been wholly successful with my mother. The truth was, he was shy with women and could never bring himself to call her Joyce, and this could make things awkward.

"My dear Mrs Jim," he said to her now, and I saw her bristle. "It is very good of you to invite me at this time of the year." She hadn't, but he held up his hand as if to ward off her words of welcome. "So you will allow me to contribute a little towards the festivities." He made a flourish towards the last piece of luggage the taxi driver had lugged into the hall. It was a hamper, a true wickerwork Christmas hamper, and it was large. "It is no more than a token, Mrs Jim, but my affection comes with it."

She had been about to give him a long, hard look, but at this she relented and called him "A wicked old rogue". She even kissed his cheek.

"Dingley Dell," he said. "This is my Dingley Dell."

"More like Tumbledown Hall," said my father, but Oscar's compliment had pleased him nevertheless. My mother had been responsible for its true name, Lane's End, for that's where it is, hidden away in a copse at the end of a farm road some miles outside town and difficult to find. Rotting thatch had let in water and it was in a bad state when we bought it. I had memories of how uncomfortable it was when I was very small, but over the years we had all three worked to make it what it was now – a suitably quaint old place for Oscar Bullimore, the writer of horror stories, to brag about where he had spent Christmas. Except that it was soon obvious, at least to me, that Oscar had not found his way to Lane's End merely for its atmosphere. Nor was it to escape London's hurly-burly. Oscar Bullimore had something else on his mind.

He was so unlike his usual self, so much on edge, that we all wondered if he was ill. Any unexpected sound from outside the house, particularly at night, made him start, but even more unusual was his reluctance to talk about himself, and, after the first mention of his new book, he did not once refer to his own writing. On top of this he made us promise not to spread the word that he was staying with us, or even that he had left London. "It is necessary," he said, "that the balm of solitude should be undisturbed." All of this meant that I would have to take great care when I wrote about him in my Christmas special for the *Courier*; in fact, I delayed telling him what I had in mind.

He did not allow his troubles to interfere with settling in. My mother teaches in Brackenridge which means that most days she gives me a lift into town in her old Fiat, which is long after my father has driven the even older Cavalier to the junction to catch his train for London. So, in the days before the holiday began, Oscar was left alone in Lane's End. He made a big effort to be helpful. Dusting and cleaning were not his forte, but food was a different matter and, when we all came home in the evening, the table was set, candles were lit, pleasant odours came from the kitchen, and at least one bottle from the hamper had been opened … and its quality tested.

"Haven't poked me nose outside all day," he'd say. "Just been sittin' by the fire readin' all your books, or writin' one of me own. Haven't seen a soul."

"You won't." My mother was more than usually busy with the Christmas groceries I'd helped her bring in. "Our mail is left in the box at the far end of the lane, and the coalman calls twice a year. That's it – isolation."

"Perfect bliss, Mrs Jim."

"It will be when term's over. Today that little devil of an angel in the nativity play shredded her wings when she tried to fly and I've got to mend them by tomorrow." She bustled out to find wire and pliers in the garage, and at last I got round to mentioning my Christmas article for the *Courier*. Nevertheless I went about it in a roundabout manner.

"Oscar," I said, "have you shown Dad your new book?"

"There'll be time enough for that, Donald." He chuckled into his wine glass. "Let's not spoil the festivities for dear old Jim."

"Has it a title?"

He lay back in his armchair, his legs crossed and one leather slipper dangling from his toes as he warmed his foot at the fire, and with one hand he balanced his glass on his round belly. He had composed himself like a jovial Christmas card and he was almost asleep. "The Handclasp of Death," he murmured.

"Ghosts?" I asked.

"Worse than that, dear boy. Much worse."

I risked another question. "So there's something particularly horrible about the handclasp, is that it?"

I already knew that Oscar would never talk of a book until it was in print – except to my father. Now I had gone too far.

"Oy," he said. "What's goin' on?" He was wide awake now, puffing through his moustache like a walrus coming up for air.

"I'm just interested," I said, but his hot little eyes were probing me so fiercely that I had to tell him the truth. "My chief wants me to write a Christmas special," I admitted. "You know, the supernatural and all that. So he naturally thought of you."

"Hmph." Oscar didn't mind that. But what I said next jerked him upright.

"So he suggested I should speak to you and—"

"What!" Red wine suddenly blotched his cardigan. "You told him I was *here*?"

It took me a while to calm him. His reaction was far too extreme for someone who was seeking only peace and quiet, and from that moment I was certain Oscar Bullimore was in hiding. Something, somewhere, terrified him.

But after a while he accepted my word that I had never given a hint to anyone that any well-known writer, let alone one as famous as Oscar Bullimore, was staying with us and I would see to it that not a word would get into print. I would lie to protect him if I had to. And all the while I was helping to blot the wine stain from his cardigan, aware of how odd it was to be scrubbing the hide of some wrinkled old monarch of the ocean who had beached himself at our fireside. But soon I noticed that the trembles in his bulk were not the result of my patting. Oscar was chuckling.

"Did I frighten 'ee, lad?" he asked.

I said I was only afraid I might have offended him.

"No son of Jim's could ever do that. I'll give you a hand with your special. A bit of 'input', as I suppose you young 'uns call it, from an old campaigner would do your piece a bit o' good, no doubt. So fill up me glass and fire away."

His skin was as thick as the leather of his fireside chair and he completely failed to see how condescending he had become, but I filled his glass to the top and got to work. What I really wanted from him was an exclusive. He was known for the elaborate secrecy that shrouded whatever it was he was working on until the moment it was published, but I aimed to lift the corner of the cloak and get him to tell me more about "The Handclasp of Death".

He huffed and puffed until his grey moustache fluttered. "You want me to reveal me secrets when it ain't half done?" He shook his head.

"You told Dad it was finished."

"Maybe I did. That was by way of being just a shade hyperbolical – your father understands."

He was squirming so I pressed him. "Just a wee hint," I urged.

"Damn the boy, he insists too much! I shall report him to his father. Did you know..." He sank into his double chins and his eyes speared me over the top of his glasses. "Has it not penetrated your immature brain that in literary matters I trust no one but Jim?" He drew in his breath. "Now would you want me to go behind the back of your dear old dad? Would you?"

"Just a hint, Oscar."

"Rat shit and pestilence! I've got a poxy journalist on me tail!"

"A hint – that's all. What does the title mean? What is 'Death's handshake'?"

"*Clasp*, you wormy little reporter. 'Hand*clasp*' – there is a difference."

He'd nibbled, so I struck. "Clasps what?"

"Another hand, of course, you poisonous oaf. Ye gods, the ignorance of the young! What does a handclasp mean other than two hands gripping … and one of them is the hand of Death." He drew in his breath. "Gloved, of course."

"Of course?" I raised my eyebrows.

"Gloved to begin with … because it is the hand of Death. You would never grasp those skeletal fingers if they were not disguised. The instant you are in that bony grip you begin the slow business of disintegration. You fall apart. Think about it, son." And the fact that Oscar himself was thinking about it was betrayed by the way he suddenly shuddered as if he was trying to shrug the idea away.

"Oscar," I said innocently, "are any of your books based on actual experiences – things that have happened to you yourself?"

He frowned as if he was seriously thinking about it, but he answered obliquely. "There are some damned nasty people around, Donald. You wouldn't want to know them."

"Do you?"

"London," he said. "That's where you find 'em. They think just because I write the stuff – I can do it!"

"Can't you?"

He glared at me. "Chopping up bodies!" he roared. "Bringing corpses back to life! Everyone knows it's all fiction, or have you gone boneheaded on me!"

There was real anger in him, but I was not going to be shaken off. "So some people believe in these things you write."

"May they rot," he said, and sank into himself, gazing into the fire.

I wanted to ask what they had done that had disturbed him so deeply, but I could see he was in no mood to tell me. "Well you won't find anyone like that around here, Oscar," I said, and I almost added: *so you've nothing to worry about.*

He snuffled noisily as he drank. "Beastly boy," he muttered, but did not object when I poured again.

"So when I write my piece for the paper," I said,

"I'll say Oscar Bullimore challenges them to risk the consequences of reading 'The Handclasp of Death'." For a moment I thought he would round on me again, so I added, "It's good publicity – it'll make 'em want to know."

He humphed again, but he'd enjoyed jousting with me. "You're a rattlesnake, Jim's boy. But as you've got what you want, you can do something for me. Will you?"

I was willing.

"You know that I always present Jim with a finished object so that he don't have to do any more than cast an eye over the spelling?" I nodded, colluding in the fantasy of Oscar's immaculate manuscript, and he went on. "Well me old Remington's packed up and the last few pages are still in me own horrible handwriting, so you can lend me your typewriter."

I have never owned a typewriter. "But you can use my computer," I said. It was a big mistake, but for a reason I could never have guessed.

5

When you see someone heading towards disaster your first urge is to haul them back, even if you don't like them. That's how I felt towards Jeremy Pyne, and I had liked him ever since his first twitchy, limp handshake. Apart from Freddie Catchpole he was the *Courier's* only full-time reporter. He was twice my age, taller, had been around a lot and spoke about his days on the nationals. Why he was now working for a country weekly was something he never mentioned but, as Freddie liked to point out, his references almost certainly said, "likes a drink". He always seemed sure of himself, yet even I could see he was walking blindfold on the edge of a long drop.

One morning we had arrived together outside the stationer's shop. "Like entering a maze, Don," he said, and tilted his narrow face towards the nameboard. The *Courier*'s title was almost squeezed out by the proprietor's name sitting on top of it. "Can hardly see there's a newspaper here – if you can call this parish mag a newspaper."

"Tell Freddie that," I said.

"I have."

And he had, even though he knew of Freddie Catchpole's burning wish to see the last of him. But Freddie had not appointed him, and the proprietor had never yet sacked anyone.

Jeremy was right about the maze. Any stranger would have found it difficult even to find the stationer's shop in the first place, hidden away as it was in a tiny back street. The feeling of being cramped into a space that was never intended for it was one of the things I liked about it. Secrets were stored here. The shop itself seemed to me to be crammed with promises – all those notebooks on display inviting you to write in them, pencils and pencil sharpeners at hand, stacks of pure white paper longing to be mated with racks and racks of pens, and every implement you could ever need to punch, staple, glue and bind your written pages into wads that riffled and could be read.

And behind all this, through a low arch, you caught a glimpse of new books with shining jackets, and, yet further into the maze and down a step, there was a dim room with an ancient carpet clogged with dust where shelves of tired old books that had long since shed their jackets leant against each other in the shadows. But even this was not the end, for there was another door, hardly visible in an alcove, with a warning sign. Staff Only, it said, and from behind it came a wheezing and subdued rattle like the breathing of great lungs.

On the day that my special article appeared I was alone when I pushed open the forbidden door and went through into the noise. I was early because the print run had not yet finished and the old flatbed press was still slowly churning out that week's issue ... with the double-page feature and my byline. I watched for a while, but it was cold standing there under the gritty skylights and I went through the cubbyhole where the printers brewed their tea and climbed the bare wooden stairs to the reporters' room. It was too early on a press day to expect anyone to be there, but the fact that the cistern of the lavatory at the top of the stairs was still trickling should have warned me.

The door of the reporters' room had hardly begun to scrape the lino when there was a shout from the darkness and the sound of a body hitting the floor. Then silence. I couldn't even hear breathing. I pushed the door a fraction further and called, "Who's there?"

No answer. I reached for the light switch.

"Don't do that, for God's sake!"

Through the gloom I could see Jeremy Pyne. His head, as narrow as a greyhound's, had lost its reckless tilt and drooped like a melting icicle. "You scared shit out of me," he said. "I was just getting my head down again – what the hell time is it?"

"Rough night, Jeremy?"

A frown folded his pale brow. "I don't remember."

"The Case is Altered?" It was a dirty little pub down by the river. For all the slender arrogance of his face, which some people considered aristocratic, Jeremy sought the low life.

"There's nowhere else." As a matter of principle he shunned all Freddie's pubs.

He stood up and began to search his pockets but was unable to prevent himself constantly listing to one side until he held his balance by wedging against his desk.

"Car keys?" I guessed what he was looking for. He nodded. "Don't worry, Jeremy, the landlord's probably still got them." It had happened before.

"Good friend of mine. Didn't want me to lose my license." He shuddered and pushed back his lank black hair. In the dimness, his hangover lit his face with a sickly whiteness. "You haven't got a cup of tea about your person, have you, Don?"

"I'll get you one from the works."

Downstairs, Jack Street, solid as cast metal under his foreman's overall, eyed me up and down and then nodded at the stairs. "Got a right one up there," he said. He had been tending the old flatbed all night and had seen Jeremy come in. "Two o'clock, stoned out of his mind. He's for the boot, ain't he?" Jack Street always wanted gossip. He ran the engine room and did not trust what went on upstairs.

"I'll get him smartened up a bit before Chiefie gets in," I said.

Jack Street's cool grey eyes did not change but something like a smile appeared below. "And you'll be for the high jump as well if *Mister* Freddie Catchpole catches you callin' him Chiefie."

"Jeremy does."

"That's what I mean. He don't keep his mouth shut when he should. Last night he was letting the whole world know what he thought of Freddie sending him out to check on a story about some bloody doctor who don't exist."

"What doctor?" But I knew.

"That one who got knocked over."

"Is there anything about it today?" I had looked at my own article in the *Courier*, nothing else.

"Don't you bloody reporters ever read your own bloody paper?"

"I didn't see anything."

"That's because it wasn't there. Freddie didn't think it was worth the space. He killed it."

Thank you, Mr Street. I went back upstairs and found Jeremy huddled beside the open window looking out into the dark alley at the back. "Thought I'd freshen the place up a bit before Chiefie's little nostrils sniff debauchery," he said. He had been warned about sleeping it off in the reporters' room. He took the tea mug in both hands and crouched over it like a refugee in a bleak landscape, but he did not miss seeing me bend over my copy of the *Courier*. We had even managed to get a picture of Oscar Bullimore by taking it from the jacket of one of his books in the shop downstairs, but nowhere in anything I had written did I give any clue that Oscar was staying with us.

"Best thing in the paper," he said. "Read it last night."

"Before you went to the pub or after?" But I was pleased.

"Cheeky young sod," he said. "Cold sober. And let me tell you something else…" He put down his mug and once more began to search his pockets, muttering to himself. "Unless I dreamt it, or was it something I only thought I saw…" But then he looked up and said, "You have a fan."

It was clear he had only hazy recollections of what had happened in the night, and he was still rummaging in his pockets when I said, "Chiefie sent you off on a wild-goose chase, didn't he?"

"Did he?" He was still searching, not listening. "There was this good-looking woman. She was coming along the alleyway last night as I came out of the back door."

"And?"

"And nothing. She wanted a copy of the *Courier*, and when I got one from the works she opened it and saw your byline, dammit. She lost all interest in me and handed me something to give to you." He fished something from his pocket. "And this is it."

He handed me a card. It was Beatrice Cole's.

"Cute little number," he said, "but a bit too old for you, I should have thought."

"She's my teacher."

"Well she wants to see you."

I shrugged. "So you didn't find him," I said, and when he looked blank I added, "The doctor in the accident – the one that Freddie..." I stopped speaking because he had ceased to hear me.

Jeremy Pyne was facing my way, but his gaze did not reach as far as me. There was something halfway between us, in the air, invisible to me but hanging there in front of him.

"A bottle!" he said. After the night he had just drunk away this could have been funny, but his lips were drawn back and his eyes did not want to see what was in front of them. I had seen him in the grip of the shakes once before, but this was worse. At that time the terror had been within him; now he was terrified by something outside himself. Something which I could not see.

"It's nothing, Jeremy," I said, and tried to persuade him that he would feel better in a minute. I took the mug from him. "I'll get you another one," I told him.

"No." But he was not talking to me. "Not a bottle. A jar. It was on the bar." The tremble in his limbs became a shudder. "It was vile!"

Now I knew what he was seeing. I had been with him to The Case is Altered and I had seen the jar. "Pickled eggs," I said.

"Eggs?" His face was contorted.

"Just eggs, Jeremy." I was struggling to get him out of the grip of the night's poison. "A few eggs are nothing to worry about."

He shook his head. "Just one," he said. "In a little jar by itself. Nothing to do with the landlord – he didn't see it."

I began to say more but he reached out and dug his fingers into my arm.

"No egg." His eyes were dull and his voice was sluggish. "Too much blood. Bloody water. And in the middle … looking straight at me, Donald … looking at me through the bloody water … it was an eye!"

6

Beaumont Villas had once been large private houses forming a terrace overlooking a public garden, but their ground floors were now solicitors' offices or dental surgeries and the upper storeys had long since been converted into flats. I climbed the steps to the door of number nine and found her name on the top bellpush.

It was quiet here. The solicitors and dentists had their cars parked in private slots against the garden railings beyond which a solitary pedestrian was walking listlessly between the trees. I did not recognize Hazel Elliott until she saw me and her face instantly brightened. I did not want her butting in, and I was calculating whether she was far enough away for me not to recognize her when the

46

door opened and Beatrice Cole made it possible for me to turn my back.

"Donald!" My teacher glanced beyond me as I entered, but I was certain she had not seen Hazel for she quickly closed the door and ushered me past the door of an antiques dealer whose rooms opened off the hallway. The dealer had not yet begun his day's business and the ground floor was dark and silent.

"It's a long way down from my flat, Donald," Beatrice Cole said as we climbed the stairs. "I'm afraid I kept you waiting out in the cold."

"It didn't worry me, Miss Cole."

The formality made her smile and she glanced sidelong at me. I reddened.

"The young lady coming across the garden," she said, her eyes still on me, "did you see her?"

"No," I answered automatically, but my guilt increased. We had both ignored her.

"I do hope it wasn't your girlfriend … she looked very much like Hazel Elliott to me."

I had to get out of this altogether. "Even if it was Hazel Elliott, she's not my girlfriend."

"Oh?" She raised her eyebrows as if my denial had been too sharp, but then her face became mischievous. "So I have made a blunder."

"I'm afraid so, Miss Cole."

"Then who *is* the lucky girl, *Mister* Price?"

She was taunting me, but her dimples were

friendly. I said, "I don't think you should ask me that question, *Miss* Cole."

She laughed and we went side by side up a staircase wide enough to show how grand the house had once been.

"Here we are." Panes of ruby glass stained the air. At night, the landing would have been a ghostly chapel, but now a ruby light swam around us and our footfalls were lost in the softness of the carpet. She paused by her door. "You are a man of mystery, Donald," she said.

I was taller, so she had to gaze up at me. I opened my mouth to speak, but we were so close that embarrassment silenced me. Her eyes widened as if something of the same sensation had reached her, and she drew in her breath so sharply it may have been a gasp as she turned away to open the door.

From coloured shadows into ordinary daylight. Her room had tall windows filled with the winter sky, and as she walked ahead of me she was my teacher once more. I strove to keep that distance. "I don't understand you," I said, and just avoided adding "Miss". "I'm not at all mysterious."

She did not respond, and walked to an elaborate marble fireplace where coals glowed in the grate. She looked over her shoulder. There was no need to do that. She could have turned around. But she looked at me over her shoulder like a girl tempting me with a secret. "What's it to be, Donald?" she asked.

I had no idea what she meant.

"Coffee?" she said. "Or something stronger?"

So that's all it was. I grinned.

"I know what that means." She went to a cabinet. "I know all you reporters like beer," once more she glanced over her shoulder, "but you'll have to make do with sherry."

She handed me a glass, poured one for herself and we stood in front of the fire. "I expect you know why I asked you here, Donald."

I could guess. The *Courier* lay on a chair opened at my article. I mumbled something.

"Surely it's unusual to have a piece with your own name on it when you have been there for such a short time," she said. "It was a thrill to see it so I couldn't resist celebrating … and here you are." She raised her glass and we drank.

I thanked her, and she stood smiling at me. She had a small mouth and the tip of her tongue touched the trace of sherry on her lips. We drank again before she took our glasses and stood them on the marble mantel.

"A toast is hardly enough," she said, and she stepped forward, raised both hands to my face, and kissed me on the lips. It was the gentlest assault possible, but it was as if she had struck me. I was so taken aback that I stood in front of her and did nothing. Her reaction was to draw back a fraction, murmur her congratulations once more, and then put her lips to mine so that we kissed in earnest. She relaxed against me, so softly yielding that I had to put my arms around her or we would have lost balance. We clung like this, dizzily, until suddenly she put her hands against my shoulders and pushed herself away.

"Oh, Donald," she said, "I *am* sorry."

I did not want to release her but she continued to push me away until it began to seem that I clung to her against her will. Awkwardly, I let her go. "It was only meant to be a peck for a good boy," she said. "You should never have turned it into something else."

So I was to blame. "I'm sorry," I said, and then tried to turn an apology into a compliment. "But it was nice." That was so clumsy and childish that I half closed my eyes in disgust at myself and watched her head droop as if she, too, was ashamed.

She did not look at me as she said, "You write well, Donald." She was struggling to be the teacher once more. "That piece in the paper shows you at your best."

"It wasn't all mine," I said. "The chief reporter gave it a bit of a tweak here and there – the crappy bits are all his." Not that I cared any longer, not with her eyes on me, and the soft rise and fall of her breasts reminding me of what had just happened.

"Newspapers," she said, "have to do things to the way you write, I suppose."

"They think they do."

She wore a plain dress of some soft, dark material that showed off the smooth, white slope of her neck. I hardly heard her when she said, "I didn't know you knew Oscar Bullimore."

"Quite well." I told her my father was his editor, and she was surprised and impressed.

"Does he admire Oscar Bullimore's work as much as I do?" she asked. This was unexpected. Oscar had his worshippers, but not many were teachers. "He's so subtle," she said.

I was surprised at that, and showed it. She moved away, and I detected that she was pretending to be more interested in Oscar Bullimore than in what was really on her mind – and mine.

"He has studied his subject." A tinge of the teacher was still there. "He knows a great deal about..." she made her fingers flutter as if she dismissed what she was about to say. "A great deal about what some people call the *black arts*."

"Too much."

She stopped moving. "What do you mean by that? Too much?"

She wanted to know, and I wanted to tell her, but I thought of Oscar sitting at home with so much fear gripping his mind that he was afraid to leave the house, and I did not want to talk of it any longer. I shrugged her question away with, "I think it gets on his mind a bit at times, that's all."

"When did you last see him?" I looked vague, but she pursued it. "Was it recently?"

"Not recently. He lives in London."

"So you had to go up to London to see him for your article."

I shook my head and she was instantly interested. "Oh, so you had to interview him somewhere else."

I would have enjoyed boasting about Oscar but her innocent questions were beginning to tempt me to give away the secret of where he was staying. "All that stuff I wrote about him is from memory," I lied. "Oscar has vanished."

"So I believe," she said. "I read it somewhere."

"Even my father has no idea where he is."

"So he's in hiding?" she asked, and when I shrugged she went on, "If you do get in touch with him, will you let me know? I would really like to help him."

I said I would, and she moved to the window. "A grey day," she said. I stood beside her and looked down into the garden. A white car was nudging its way along the road looking for a parking space. "It's so cold and bleak out there," she said, "and no one knows where poor Oscar is hiding."

"Maybe he's just gone somewhere for a break; nobody knows that he's actually in hiding."

She was watching the car, but when it drifted off round a corner she turned to me. "Nobody knows?" There was a smile on her lips. "Not even you?"

"Why me?"

"You are a deep one, Donald. You know more than you say." To prevent me denying it she reached up quickly and kissed me. "A real peck this time," she said. "Now off you go." But by then I was pulling her close. "Stop!" She pushed against me, twisting in the circle of my arms. I had gone too far again and I was about to release her when suddenly she froze and drew in her breath. She was gazing down into the road. The white car had reappeared and was easing into a space, but it could not have been that which held her attention and made her shrink close as if to hide herself behind me. It was then, with Beatrice Cole's head against my chest, that I saw what she saw. Hazel Elliott was in the garden gazing up at us.

Shame made her drive me out of her flat. "Don't come back," she pleaded as I stood in the dusky red light of the landing. She was nervous of what neighbours might say … and afraid of what one of her pupils had seen from the garden below. "You must leave. Don't let anyone see you." She shut the door.

Downstairs I stepped quickly past the door of the antique dealer's office and looked out into the street. Trees hid the garden behind the railings and Hazel was nowhere in sight. Further along the road the white car was hidden among the others. No one had got out so I moved swiftly down the steps and walked in the other direction so that no one should see me leave.

7

We finished early on press day. I couldn't get a lift so I had to cycle home under a bitter sky so dark it brought an early dusk. The journey was cold, the frozen gravel of the drive barely broke up under my feet, and when I put my key in the door it refused to turn. It had happened before. My mother, last one out of the house in the morning, had locked it on the inside and left by the back door.

I trudged around the house, my mind full of Beatrice Cole. She had told me to go away and not return, but her face had been so full of regret and she had closed the door with such a gentle reluctance that I was eager to get indoors and ring her without the risk of being overheard. I reached into the woodshed where the back-door key hung on a nail. It was not there. I sighed, and stood back to see if any window gave me a hope of climbing in. And then my heart lurched and missed a beat.

On the upper floor a watcher had moved back into the blackness of a room. My parents' bedroom. I was looking around for a weapon when my head suddenly sagged. I was a fool. Thinking about Beatrice Cole had driven Oscar Bullimore out of my head. Then alarm jerked my head up. Why was the house so dark, no light in any room?

I moved further back to get a better view of the window. "Oscar!" I shouted, and then louder, "Oscar!"

I was reaching for an axe in the woodshed when the door of the house rattled and Oscar's voice reached me. "For God's sake keep quiet!"

I had the axe. "Are you all right? Is there anyone there?"

"I'm alone. And keep your voice down, will you?" From the shadow of the doorway he saw what I was holding. "Good idea," he said. "Bring it with you."

I must have been a menacing sight for he backed away as I came forward, and it was up to me to switch on the light when I was inside. We stood blinking at each other and I saw that he also was armed, with the brass poker from the living room.

"Alone are you?" He was wheezily anxious. "Quite alone?"

I nodded.

"Thought so. I've been watching you all around the house."

"That's why you were in my mother's room."

"What?" That alarmed him even more. "Oh my God – yes. That's where I was." He blew out his moustache, and it would have been comical except that his plump cheeks were mottled, unhealthy with fear. "My dear chap, I was in your parents' room. Quite unforgivable. But I had to keep watch on you, do you see? Not snooping, I swear."

Someone had to make a move. I put down the axe, and he noticed the poker in his own hand. "Had a bit of a fright," he mumbled. "I'll put it back ... back where I got it. Living room, that's right," and he led the way. He was standing by the fireplace when he suddenly stiffened. "You did lock the back door, didn't you, old son?"

The mystery had gone on long enough. "What's been happening, Oscar?"

He became shifty, unable to meet my eye, and was silent for a long moment. When he spoke he mumbled as if he didn't want me to hear. "Haven't been altogether square with you, old friend. Badly need forgiveness." I stayed silent. He cleared his throat. "Abused the hospitality of the house," he growled and swung towards me as though I was the one at fault. "Been prying into your papers ... private papers of a gentleman kind enough to give a poor old dimwit the use of –" he sought for the word – "the use of his electric machinery."

"My computer," I said.

"That's the brute."

It was the first one he had ever operated and he had been singing its praises. "But I thought you loved it, Oscar."

"Too much, old son, too much. That devil's device gave away your secrets, spilled them out like a god-damned traitor."

This time it was me who could not meet his eyes. What had I written that shamed me? What secret file had he stumbled on? My mind raced as feverishly as the flames flickering in the grate.

"I don't wonder at you keeping silent." Oscar was shamefaced. "You never meant me to poke around and find it, but I swear to God I only pressed a button and it threw the whole damn thing in me face!"

"What, Oscar? What did it tell you?"

For the first time he looked at me steadily. "The severed finger," he said.

My mind raced again. The story that never was. I had made notes on the screen but common sense had told me that the finger had been a pig's knuckle-bone and my imagination, so I had never printed it out.

"All true?" he asked.

"I thought so at the time," I said, and he grunted and put the poker down in the hearth.

"Your dear old dad wouldn't begrudge me a drink," he said, and he went to the sideboard and poured himself a whisky. He raised his eyebrows at me, I nodded once more, and he poured another.

"Long life," he said.

"Long life."

We drank.

I told him all I knew, making light of it but excusing my gullibility by saying that "a girl I knew" had been guilty of the same hallucination and this had made it all the more believable – at the time. But at every attempt I made to laugh it off he held up his hand to prevent me, so that as I spoke I became aware of my own voice rising and falling, and of the dark house around us and the bleak night taking possession of the fields and empty lanes that hemmed us in. When I had finished I said what was obvious: "So that's why you locked yourself in today."

"I never knew until I saw it on your machine," he said. "I never knew they were so close at hand!" He shook his head to prevent me asking who *they* were, got to his feet and downed his glass in one. He was at the sideboard pouring another before he spoke again.

"Heard of 'The Skinners'?" he asked. "No, of course you haven't – no one has; I've seen to that."

"It was one of your first stories," I said.

My knowledge gave him a shock. "How on

earth…!" His mouth opened and shut. "Where did you see it?"

"I haven't seen it; I just know about it."

"How?"

"Your bibliography," I said. My father had been working on a list of all Oscar's writings and I had helped him check it. " 'The Skinners' was a short story in some little magazine my father had heard about."

Oscar shut his eyes. The fingers holding his drink became so white I thought his glass would shatter. "He has betrayed me! I told him it did not exist. I disown it, I reject it … I have sent it to hell!"

"But Dad got to know someone who had a copy. He read it."

"Did you?"

"I've never set eyes on it, Oscar." All I knew was that it was a story about a murderous cult who believed that by wrapping themselves in the skin of their victims they increased their powers over others.

"And…?" said Oscar, but that was as far as my knowledge went. He looked down at the floor as if he was reluctant to continue, but then he spoke gruffly. "It went a stage further than that, Donald. They discovered that once they were even partially clothed in the skin of their victims they had control over that part of the body they had flayed." He raised his head and opened his eyes wide as though startled at what he was telling me.

He was speaking as though this was no longer a story he had invented, but a fact. He was very much my senior, but I found myself trying to ease him out of his delusions. "It's a completely hideous idea, Oscar," I said, but I was grinning, complimenting him on the stretch of his imagination. "It's utterly gross. Who'd have thought a nice man like you could have a mind as nasty as that?"

It was a line that had brought a smirk to the face of every author I'd got to know, but Oscar hung his head and all the life in him seemed to drain away in a long sigh. I tried to raise his spirits. "I don't see why you want to suppress the story," I said. "A lot of people would admire it."

But Oscar's mind was on something else. "Have you ever heard of L'Aube Noire?" he asked.

My French was good enough for that. "The Black Dawn?" I said. "Could mean a rainy daybreak, I suppose."

"Blacker by far than that," said Oscar. "Black Dawns came up over the gallows whatever the weather." He squinted at me over his glasses to see what effect that had. "And did you know that the hangman was allowed to sell the rope, and that people paid good money for it? And did you know that, if he had made the drop too big so that the neck of his client was stretched a bit too far so that his skin was torn, the bloodied rope put more cash in his hand – did y'know that?"

I had heard of it, but he had switched from hanging to something else.

"So just think," he said, "of the profit an executioner could make from the spillage of the guillotine."

"France," I said, but I had no idea where this was leading.

"France," he repeated. "Bits of cloth dipped in blood and worth money. Strange currency ... but there's more to it than that." He fixed me with a glare that kept me quiet. "I've been in this writing game a long time, Donald, so I've done me researches and I know that deep in France in one of those villages perched high up on steep hillsides there was an aristocrat who had a reputation as a necromancer ... and much more and much worse. But the name he came to be known by seemed innocent enough. For miles around he was known as the Marquis de Terre Cuite, Lord Terra Cotta, because one of his many passions was pottery. In his chateau high above the village he had his kilns and his furnaces where he fired his pots, and some damn strange things came out of 'em. I know he made at least one coffin, shaped like a man, and the village people said a human being was baked inside it so that it would not collapse inside the kiln. Nice feller, the old Marquis.

"Came the Revolution, and the Marquis de Terre Cuite met his end. Like a lot of other aristos he was swept away by the Terror and came to the guillotine. Got what he deserved, but that wasn't the end of it. Oh no, not at all. One of his cronies, who knew all his little secrets, hid under the scaffold to collect his precious blood, and he heard the last words uttered by the Marquis ... after his head was cut off! The tale goes that when the executioner held the head up to show the populace it whispered 'Vive l'Aube Noire'!

"Poppycock, Donald? Maybe, but I reckon that there was a sound even if it was only the whistle of air from the severed windpipe of the corpse. It happens, dear boy, and that's how stories begin and get carried on... The Black Dawn still exists."

In spite of the grimness of the story – or maybe because he sensed that I was sceptical – Oscar smiled. "Not much left of the old chateau. Been there in me travels and there's nothing but a few walls and the kilns have crumbled to dust. But someone had dug up one of those coffins and it stands there just like a damn great pastry man ... gives you a bit of a turn, propped up against a bit of old stonework, lookin' at you." He looked at the floor and growled, "Just wish I'd never set eyes on the blasted thing, that's all."

He fell silent, but I could not let it end there. I said, "I should have thought it was just up your street, Oscar."

"That's the trouble – it was!" He raised his head. "I used some of it in that story, and I rue the day that Jim ever jogged me memory and brought it to my mind!"

I could not understand how my father came into it, and said so, but Oscar only grumbled about how Jim had long ago overheard some kids in Brackenridge talking about a "scary statue" that someone's father had seen in a house somewhere in the county, and this had set Oscar's mind working. "So I wrote 'The Skinners'," he said. "Can't blame your dear old dad for it, though; it was long before he became me editor and I never showed it to him. There's others to blame for what has happened."

A rattle of sleet against the window-pane alarmed him. He made me put out the light and we padded from room to room, listening and looking until he was convinced that nothing was prowling around the house. When we got back to the fireside he refused to switch on the light but sat there, drinking steadily. "Somethin' happened a few weeks ago," he said suddenly. "A girl, a young woman, I don't know how old, rang me up and asked if I could give her and a few of her chums a bit of a talk about me work. Seems it had given 'em all a bit of a thrill, so I could hardly say no, could I?"

"Hardly." Oscar was as sweet as roly-poly pudding when he was surrounded by his fans. "But who were they?"

"Wish to God I knew, boy. I wouldn't be here now if I'd been able to pin them down." He rubbed his forehead and gazed into the flames. He was still perturbed but the blotchiness had left his cheeks. "I met them, but I couldn't recognize one of 'em today, not even the young woman who came to pick me up ... because she was wearing a mask. Didn't worry me because I've seen that sort of stuff many a time; little groups actin' the part – y'know the sort of thing."

I nodded. Oscar collected a clientele like that.

"Little house in Hampstead, that's where she took me. Somewhere not far from Keats Grove, poky little place, but I had the feeling they weren't exactly on home territory, know what I mean? Little bit unfamiliar with the set-up. But at the time I thought it was all part of the act. All smiles they were, what I could see of their faces; well they would be, wouldn't they, butterin' me up so's I wouldn't charge 'em for it.

"But there was something fishy from the start – even the smell of that house. I was afraid it was the cookin' at first, and then I thought there was just the outside edge of incense to it, although it wasn't too appetising, and I said to meself: ho-ho-ho I know what's goin' on here, Bullimore, old son, somethin' exotic. And I wouldn't have minded, either, because the flame is not yet dead in this fat frame, Donald, and to tell you true I sensed there was enough female pulchritude in that room to bring back the stirrings of yesteryear. They'd kept everything pretty dim, only a candle or two for the sake of the atmosphere, and I have to say they were more than civil about me work, leading me on about this and that, but all the time workin' their way into that damned tale I wrote…"

He wouldn't name it, and I said nothing.

"The tale you know of. And they had been getting me to agree that there's always a degree of truth in whatever you write, no matter how unlikely … or even downright blasted impossible. So when we came to that particular story the questions came thick and fast. All about skin and its texture, how it always had to reflect what lay beneath it so it was the outward manifestation of the inner body. They were saying outright that skin just had to be magical stuff as on one side it was connected to the air we breathe, but on its hidden side it had roots in our inner workings.

"And then they got on to the bit in the story where I'd worked in the old Marquis and his pottery. The terracotta coffin was their big thing… They'd worked on it and tied it up in all sorts of ways I'd never thought of – like the essence of the man who was baked to death was still in the coffin, and how it could be absorbed by anything that lay in that coffin for a certain length of time, and that the skin in particular would have special properties.

They'd worked it all out in their own minds, Donald – exactly how long it would take, what fluids were necessary, what parts of the body would be best for their experiments…

"And all this guff was in *my* story. Marvellous, Mr Bullimore, wonderful! I was the prophet who'd led the way, and this little gathering was to honour me."

He blew out his cheeks, himself again, and sat back in his chair. "It was all a bit of a knock-out … but I'd had this sort of thing before, as your dad knows, but nothin' anything like on this scale. And then…" He broke off before he drew in his breath and went on, "And then someone brought in the rat."

The blotches had returned to his cheeks. I reached for his glass and went to the sideboard for a refill. Both of us were listening to the wind that moaned softly round the house – if it was the wind. I knew what was on his mind so I said, "I'll go and look." It was black outside and I could see nothing, because there was nothing there; I was certain of it. "All clear," I told him.

"I never once saw him clearly, did you know that?"

"The rat?" I had no idea where his mind was taking him.

"Oh, my God, I saw that all right! No, it was the feller in the corner who'd been keepin' himself to himself all evening, but now they switched on a spotlight right alongside me and I was so dazzled that when he came forward, even if he hadn't been wearing a mask like the rest of 'em, I couldn't have told him from a baboon's backside." Oscar leant forward. "This feller came towards me out o' the shadows, and as he did so I realized what the horrible cookin' smell was. It wasn't fish, and it wasn't incense, and it wasn't a *substance* – it was formaldehyde; that horrible sickly stuff they use for preserving things. And this geezer reeked of it."

I was still in what I knew of Oscar's story. This man had been experimenting on himself. I opened my mouth but Oscar knew what was in my mind. He shook his head.

"No," he said. "Not that. It wasn't him … it was what he brought with him. The smell came from a little, flat enamel dish which he put down in front of me on the table. It had a cloth over it and, without a word, he pulled it back. It damn near made me puke." Oscar bared his teeth as he screwed up his face. "There was this rat … and they'd skinned it! Pink and white and blue it was, swillin' around in that formaldehyde muck."

He broke off and I began to say something, but he put up his hand to stop me.

"Worse," he said. "This feller put his hand in his pocket and he brought out another rat – a live one, and I got out of me seat and began to back away because I didn't want to see what was going to happen next. I wanted no part of it, but he began strokin' the damn thing and told me no harm would come to it, so I sat down and watched him. It was then I saw he wasn't really strokin' it at all; he had got hold of the skin of the dead one and was fittin' it over the live one!"

I grunted with disgust and he fixed me with his hot little eyes for a moment and nodded. Wait, he was telling me, there's more.

"He put the rat down on the table next to the dish. I didn't want it anywhere near me, I can tell you, Donald, but I did manage to see they'd fixed that skin over it with elastic bands or somethin'. It didn't seem to mind, and what he did next you'd have thought was kind and natural except for everything else. He fed it. He put scraps of something in front of it and then he took his hands away out of the light and left the rat there nibbling away to its heart's content."

He looked at me, and I looked at him.

"And that's all?" I asked.

"Nothin' happened, Donald. I just sat there in that little ring of light, and all around me everyone was quiet and watching. I could feel that they were waiting, and then they let out one damn great sigh, all together as though they'd rehearsed it. For a moment I couldn't see what was so satisfying to them, but then, in the white dish, I saw a movement. That skinned rat had opened its blasted mouth! I saw it gnawing away at the air, and its paw moved as if it was turning something over ... just as the other rat did the same! 'What the hell,' I said, 'have you got it wired up, or something?' "

Oscar shook his head as though answering himself. "No, they told me, it wasn't a trick. It was something they'd learnt from my story ... how to distill the juices until they'd extracted the essence of the dead creature and then transfer it by means of the skin to something living. They'd done it, they'd showed me they could do it, and they'd scared me out o' me wits."

I waited. He seemed to have finished. He drank. "And then they told me what they called themselves." He looked at me and raised his eyebrows. "You know what that was, don't you?"

"The Black Dawn," I said softly.

He was equally quiet. "Spot on, Donald. L'Aube Noire, and they still followed the necromantic beliefs of the old Marquis ... to the point, they told me, of brewing something inside one of the pots they'd filched from the ruins of his chateau. Are you with me, Donald?"

I nodded. Our eyes held for a long moment before he spoke.

"And then it happened," he said.

A couple of the people in the background had come forward and had taken away the living rat and the dead rat. And then the one who seemed to be their leader had produced a parcel. "It was something quite well wrapped up," said Oscar, "about half the length of your arm, and quite limp." He shut his lips tight thinking of the right word. "Half the length of your arm ... and soggy. Wrapped in a green sheet but slightly discoloured at one end, as if something had oozed. But it just lay there on the table with this feller sittin' beside it. All I saw were his hands and arms and he was going to do something with this thing because he started putting on a glove. It looked like a surgeon's glove, whitish, but either it didn't fit him or it was a bit flimsy because he was having trouble. Hell's bells, Donald boy, I was leaning forward to help him when I saw this glove had no fingertips, at least not where the nails would have been ... and of course it didn't," Oscar's voice got louder and he rose to his feet, "because that was no damned glove he was fitting on, it was the skin of a human hand!"

He was so filled with revulsion as he relived that moment that he stood glaring down at me as though he was in a fury with me. "What did you do?" I said.

"I got out. What the hell do you think I did! I asked 'em where the bathroom was, and then before they knew it I was out in the street." He flung his head back and filled his lungs, just as though he had made his escape again. "And I had a bit o' luck. Just a couple of doors away there was a police car at the kerb, doing nothin', having a tea break or something, so I told this young copper what was going on and he dived into this house double quick."

Oscar was heading for the sideboard at speed. "So what did he find?" I said to his back.

"Nothin'," he grunted. "Not a bloody thing. I hung around while that young copper went pokin' around inside, and when he came out he said he'd drawn a blank, but they'd be sending round a squad to make sure. And then he called up a cab for me and sent me home." He spun around. "But they're after me, Donald! I've had threats!"

"What sort of threats?"

At this he became shifty, unable to meet my eye and give an explanation. Suddenly I saw him as an old man whose mind had gone. Too much imagination, too much flattery and too much drink had undone him. And I was partly to blame. My own imagination had set a finger walking, and his chance discovery of this had triggered what was already working within his brain.

"Phone calls?" I asked. "Have you had phone calls?"

"That's it, Donald." He was mumbling. "Nasty phone calls."

"Then you should tell the police."

"For God's sake!" He was suddenly looming over me, threatening. "They're part of it! I rang 'em up again and spoke to this same young copper. They searched the place from top to bottom and said they found nothing. But there was something there — there had to be! You can't do things like that with a human body without leaving a trace!"

Car tyres crunched the gravel. My mother was home; soon my father would arrive from the station.

"Say nothin'!" It was half an order, half a plea. "You're the only one I can trust, Donald. Don't say a word, or I'm done for!"

8

That night, with four of us around the table, Oscar's fears dropped away. He sat there in his plum-coloured waistcoat with his face to match, mopping his forehead with the spotted handkerchief – his bandanna, as he called it – that always dangled from his top pocket, and he even began to drop hints that he and I had a secret.

My father, who had had to deal with Oscar in all his moods, was quietly amused by his bragging, but my mother was becoming more and more exasperated. She put down her fork. "Oscar," she said, "what's going on?"

"Madam?" He cocked a bleary eye.

"Don't you madam me, you old villain. What's going on between you two?"

"Mrs Jim," he said, ruffling her even more, "to tell the secrets of my prison house I could a tale unfold, the lightest word of which would harrow up thy soul…"

"Prison house?" She ended his theatricals, but managed to laugh. "It's *you* who's turning this house into a prison … it's as though you are afraid to go out."

"But that's just it, Mrs Jim – I am!"

My father butted in. "Oscar Bullimore afraid?" he said. "It's got to be something pretty fearsome."

A placid man, my father, but he could always puncture bluster when he had to. Now Oscar had to tell all, or back down. I was already wincing for him when he tilted his red face towards me and gazed at me over his peculiar little spectacles.

"What do you think, Donald?" he said. "Should I tell 'em?"

I was uncomfortable. If he told them his part of the story mine would be sure to come out and I would be made to look foolish. But I would be more foolish if I tried to stop him. "It's up to you, Oscar."

"I want you to do something for me, Donald." He spoke gravely. "But before that I must make certain that your mother and father understand why I make my request." His spectacles glinted at me and then at them as he informed them not about our true secret but that he was sending me to town to replenish the supplies of wine that he had helped to drink. And I was commissioned to purchase "a little extra" as a token for Christmas. Then, with a wave of the hand to brush away any protest, he handed me a blank cheque. He became more solemn. "I would wish to go into town myself, but I am prevented from doing so because I am being pursued –" he drew in his breath – "by people from the city." He paused for emphasis. "Very nasty people."

"Debt collectors," said my father. The gesture of the blank cheque had not impressed him, and he knew his authors. He didn't even blush. Oscar, on the other hand, was indignant.

"Worse!" he exclaimed. "Fans!"

My mother, who thought it was expected of her, laughed. But there was no hint of humour on Oscar's face. He spoke directly to me. "I have been telling Donald how a group of my –" he cleared his throat – "admirers have taken to stalking me." He swung away to address my mother. "Every step I take! Day and night! There they are!"

There was so much urgency in the way he spoke that she took him seriously. "You are quite safe here, Oscar, surely."

"No, madam, I am not. Your son has evidence that they are lurking nearby. Someone wants my autograph."

At last I twigged what he was doing. He was

covering what he took to be the truth of his predicament with this talk of ardent fans. Even if he was out of his mind, it had done nothing to ruin his cunning. In spite of myself I was about to back him up when my father did what he could to spoil it.

"I thought it was every author's dream, Oscar," he said. "I'll give head office a ring and we'll arrange a book-signing while you're here."

"No!" It was a roar. "On no account. My life is in danger!"

"Torn apart by lady admirers," my mother said. "Not a bad way to go."

"Please, Mrs Jim… I mean Joyce." It was a mark of how earnest he had become. "Please don't make light of it. Tell no one I am here. Even the slightest word would put them on to me."

"Not even in the staffroom at school?"

He was aghast. "You haven't," he pleaded. "For heaven's sake tell me you haven't."

"Well, as a matter of fact…" she dragged it out, tormenting him, "I haven't had the chance, yet."

His face had become so haggard that she had to reassure him and swear she would tell no one. My father had had no contact with anyone in town since Oscar descended on us, and at work he had been so hectically busy with other matters that Oscar Bullimore had not been mentioned. For once, Oscar was pleased to hear it.

* * *

Next morning I plumed the air with my breath as I sped through the frosted sparkle of white lanes, felt the sun on my neck and the rasp of air on my face and let it scour yesterday out of my mind.

In just a few months I seemed to have lost touch with most of my friends. Work was to blame. Everyone around me on the *Courier* was older than me and I had entered their country. They did things differently there. Why should I be shrouded by their clouded minds, or caught up in the jumbled nightmares of people who drank too much? Oscar was one, and there was also Jeremy Pyne. I picked up speed and let them both dissolve in the air behind me with all the rest.

Except one. Beatrice Cole. She was why I was hurrying to work. No one knew that my mind was filled with Beatrice Cole. Even when Oscar Bullimore was telling me of a rat in a tray of formaldehyde, or of a glove made of human skin, my brain lingered in a rose-coloured corridor and the first soft touch of her body. I would ring her, with any excuse to see her.

I was early and once more the office was deserted, but I had not been forgotten. Nor had Christmas. There was a large sepia photograph on my desk with a note from Freddie Catchpole. The picture showed a butcher's shop at a Christmas long ago, and the shop was almost invisible behind row after row of turkeys and pheasants strung across its front. The present owner's grandfather, wearing his striped apron, stood outside this feathered cloak, and Freddie thought it would make "a nice little story for the festive season".

I pushed it aside, but then thought I could spend the whole morning chasing it when I was really with my teacher. More festive than Freddie could imagine.

I rang her, and that was the first disappointment of the day. There was no answer. She would be at school; I had forgotten that. Nevertheless I wandered around to Beaumont Terrace and rang the bell of her flat. She was not at home. A perfect chance had gone to waste and I was not in a good temper when I wandered towards the market place to interview the butcher. But his shop was crowded and I had no urge to interview him among a press of customers and the smell of meat.

I was turning away when I remembered I had Oscar's cheque in my pocket. I would go to the wine shop and Oscar would regret he'd left the cheque blank; I was in the mood to cane him. There was a blue sky, a nip in the air, and I was hurrying along the path in a brighter frame of mind when I realized I was walking behind Hazel Elliott.

She was about to cross the road, but hesitated at the edge of the pavement. She wore jeans and had her hands in the pockets of her short jacket. Different clothes; a different girl. But she stood there uncertainly and seemed sad and lonely. I was on the point of speaking to her, but changed my mind and was about to lose myself inside the wine shop when she turned and recognized me. Her face brightened and we traded smiles, but just as suddenly her eyes clouded and she dipped her head. I knew what had happened. She had remembered me and Beatrice Cole at the window. Now, however, I could not ignore her, and as I approached she blushed wildly as though she had been the one at fault, not me.

"It's cold," I said crassly.

"Yes." But now she was pale, even her lips. I noticed that her mouth turned down slightly at the corners, and that her eyes were too large and too grey. They made me feel guilty, and I could not forgive her for them.

I glanced away. It was not a market day, and the market place was filled with parked cars. The wine shop would be my escape route and I was about to say I had to go when, beyond the frosted rooftops of the cars, I caught a glimpse of something that, in spite of myself, made me say "Look!" and point.

I had spotted a man as he came out of an alleyway and walked towards the cars. Now he was among them and all we could see was his hat, the brim pulled down to hide his face. I recognized it.

"It's him," I said.

She was bewildered, and now the hat was no longer visible over the car rooftops. I heard an engine start. Some idea of having the help of a witness made me tug at Hazel Elliott's arm, and together we jinked through the lines of vehicles just as the car was accelerating away. There was a blurred glimpse of a waxy face and he was gone.

"Missed him!" I was trying to read the number plate, but it was impossible. "He's the one," I said. "The man who was knocked down – the doctor." Her mouth was open, and her eyes searched my face stupidly. "It's him," I insisted. "There was a girl with him and she told me who he was. He's Dr Goodwin!"

She shook her head. "No, he's not."

"I recognize him. He's the man … Dr Goodwin."

"I know him," she said. "His name is not Goodwin … and he's not a doctor."

9

Hazel Elliot was shy. Maybe I rushed her too much, but she was my only proof someone calling himself Doctor Goodwin existed, and I had to let Freddie Catchpole know I had traced him. So I took her with me to the *Courier* office.

If it hadn't been for the manageress behind the counter of the stationer's shop, Hazel would have run away before we got through the door. But the instant the doorbell jangled, Phyllis Lightfoot came hurtling forward, all angles and elbows and smiling at me as though she was my mother and I was bringing home a girlfriend for the first time.

"And you are?" she said, stooping like a sunflower towards Hazel. "I've seen you around

82

town such a lot, but your name quite escapes me." And she beamed as though this was a huge compliment.

Hazel told her, and Phyllis was delighted. "Now I have you!" she cried. "Your mother is Mrs Elliott of Barton Overhill, that's right? Lovely village right up there in the hills."

"It's very small," Hazel whispered.

"And all the better for that. I met your mother at the garden fête, and I believe I caught a glimpse of you at the same time."

More than likely. Phyllis put together a page in the *Courier* every week with reports from the villages. As she also managed the shop no one thought of her as a reporter, although she knew twice as many people as Freddie, could type quicker and never made a mistake. Now she and Hazel were talking about Barton Overhill and the scandal of it having no bus service because it was too small, and I was getting impatient. She saw it and asked, "So are you going through to the press office?" I nodded and she said to Hazel, "This young man always has *pressing* business." It was her joke, and Hazel smiled and blushed.

"We've got a story for Freddie," I said. Hazel was going to be my evidence.

"That old ogre. He and Jeremy Pyne have been snarling at each other all morning."

"So what's new, Phyllis?"

"Nothing, Donald. But just you see that you protect this young lady in that den of lions."

I had to give Hazel points for the way she raised her chin as if she did not care, but her smile was an uncertain flicker. Phyllis shepherded us through the shelves of stationery into the second-hand books section. Behind Hazel's back, she nodded first at Hazel and then at me and mouthed, "She's nice", but I frowned and shook my head. That was the trouble of being anywhere near a girl when an old matchmaker like Phyllis was around. Her motherly smile would have burned away if she had known where my thoughts really lay. Nevertheless there was some pleasure in guiding a girl through the foreign country of the print works, up the narrow clatter of the stairs and into the tired shambles of the reporters' room. I felt I had to protect her against what she might find there, and Freddie Catchpole and Jeremy Pyne did not let me down.

They sat with their backs to each other, a couple of world-weary, disgruntled old journalists that nobody's mother would want her child to know. Freddie punched a typewriter, and Jeremy had his overcoat collar turned up and did not trouble to turn our way. He seemed to be asleep. I glanced at Hazel and shrugged. She was uneasy, but she managed to look around and wrinkle her nose at the whole set-up.

"Freddie," I said, loudly enough to stop his racket. "You remember that story about the doctor we couldn't trace?"

He was still concentrating on his copy, hardly listening.

"The man who was knocked down." I reminded him of the story he had killed and which I was just about to revive. He looked round, saw Hazel, and put two and two together. "Ah, Miss," he said. "So you are the nurse who was with him."

"No, Freddie. That was a different girl. Older." Wasn't everybody older than us? I was losing patience with them all. "This is Hazel Elliott. She knows the man."

"Good." Freddie nodded his thanks to her, then turned to me. "Give him a ring and find out how he is." He returned to his keyboard and I glowered at his back.

"Freddie. There's more to it than that." His typing paused. "They lied to me. They gave a false name."

I had gained his attention but all he said was, "It happens."

I didn't give up. "And he isn't even a doctor. That's another lie."

"So what *is* his name?"

"Slade. He lives out at Barton Overhill."

There was a smirk on Freddie's face. "So if you were Mr Slade from out there at Barton Overhill and you had come into town on market day with your girlfriend, had a slight accident with a bus and got to your feet just as some young spark from the paper came up to you, asking questions that were going to get you into trouble with your wife, wouldn't you want to get rid of him – give him a name, any name, to shake him off?"

I began to protest, but he held up a hand.

"He wasn't hurt," he said. "The story's dead." The keys drummed again and I left the room, muttering under my breath.

Hazel was apologizing even before we got to the foot of the stairs. "I'm so sorry, Donald. It's all my fault."

"Forget it." I had just been humiliated.

"But it wouldn't have happened, Donald, if I hadn't made so much fuss." I was the one who had made the fuss. She had done nothing wrong.

We faced each other in the gloom of the second-hand book room. "Donald," she said quietly, "have I got you into trouble?"

"I'm used to it," I said. "Freddie's always like that."

"But he's wrong, Donald." She was using my name too often; it was a kind of flattery but I don't think she was aware of it. "There's something going on, and it isn't right you should be pushed aside."

"What do you mean – something's going on? Where?"

Suddenly she could not meet my eyes. "It's Mr Slade," she said, and fell silent.

"What about him?"

"It's what people in the village think. They don't like him."

"Why not?"

"Because he keeps to himself too much and won't have anything to do with them." She knew she was just passing on village gossip, and she heard me sigh. "He does have people go there, but they're all the same, nobody sees them in the village. And Mr Catchpole can say what he likes about him giving a false name so that his wife shouldn't get to know he was with that girl, but he doesn't have a wife and that girl is always in his house ... as far as anyone knows."

Her voice fell away. It was all pretty lame, and she knew it.

"So you think I should find out a lot more – not let the story drop. Is that what you're telling me?" I was being more aggressive than I intended.

"Oh," she said, but it was more like a gasp and there was an awkward silence between us when there were footsteps and Jeremy came into the book room.

"Chiefie's in form," he said. His grin was solely for Hazel. I was ignored. "You have just seen our master at his best. Magnificent, wasn't he?" He introduced himself, something I should have done earlier. Worse than that, he suggested we should find a place where we could drink Freddie's health. Hazel glanced at me, made an assumption that she was not wanted, and said it was time she had to go.

We parted outside the shop, and as we watched her leave Jeremy said to me, "Lucky young devil."

"You've got it wrong about her and me, Jeremy."

"Is that a fact?" He looked sidelong at me for a long moment. "Well, in that case, you'll be free tonight."

"Maybe."

"Care to give me a hand with something?"

"Doing what?"

"Chasing a story, what else."

"I'm not sure." I was thinking of Beatrice Cole.

"Chiefie's right," Jeremy raised his eyes to the sky, "you're useless. Here am I, chasing up a story that could set Chiefie's arse alight and I'm asking for your help – but you, you silly young sod, are not sure!"

"Put like that, Jeremy, how could I refuse?"

"Well, I'll see you in the pub by the river tonight. There's something going on and I need an extra pair of eyes."

There it was again, "something going on" and I was being dragged into it. "An extra pair of eyes," I repeated. "Can't you get them in a bottle?"

It was a cruel thing to say, and Jeremy gave me a long, hard look. "You think I'm joking," he said, and the outcome was that I agreed to meet him in The Case is Altered. Given half a chance, however, I would see Beatrice Cole; at least I knew where I stood with her.

10

Freddie had a copy of the *Courier* spread out on his desk and was marking items with his pernickety red pen. I knew what was coming. The *Courier* would land on my desk with his instructions to clip the items he had marked and file them. I got out.

"Oh!" The startled feminine cry made me realize I had been in too much of a rush as I got to the foot of the stairs and pushed open the door of the second-hand book room.

"I'm sorry," I said and advanced cautiously into the dimness. "I didn't expect there'd be anyone here."

I could see no one. "Hello," I said.

"I'm over here." A shadow stirred in an alcove among the shelves. "You seem in a big hurry."

The single light-bulb in the centre of the room made many a dark corner. "Is that you?" I asked the darkest.

"Of course it is, if it's me you're after."

"You can't be reading in there. It's too dark."

"Almost. But not quite."

I went forward. The scent in the alcove was the scent I had met on the rose-coloured landing. I stepped inside it.

"Very few people know about this place," I said. "Did you find anything you want?"

"It's possible." Beatrice Cole had a book in her hands.

"It's very rare to find anything you want in here."

"Have *you* found anything, Donald?"

"I have." I paused. "And what have you found?"

"You'd be surprised." She made no attempt to show me the book. "But I mustn't delay you, Donald."

"Why not?"

"Because you are chasing a story, I expect." She sounded as if she was smiling. "Hot on the trail of someone or other."

"Getting close." I played along with her. "Very close."

We fell silent. In the grainy dimness of the alcove it was impossible to be certain of her expression.

"Well," I said, not moving. "I suppose I'd better be on my way."

"To meet your girlfriend?"

"What girlfriend?"

"The girl from Barton Overhill, of course."

"You even know where she comes from." Neither of us had mentioned Hazel by name.

"I see her from time to time," said Beatrice Cole. "She seems very interested in you."

"Whoever she may be."

Beatrice Cole smiled. "She's very shy, so she must be keen … unless there's something else involved."

"And what would that be?" I asked.

"How would I know?" She smiled again, taunting me. "But I would think that any young man would find her adorable."

I wanted to ask her why she was so interested in Hazel Elliott; could it be that she was jealous? I did not have the nerve to ask so I shrugged and changed the subject. "Will you have a coffee with me?" There was a hotel on the market place.

"Better not." She could have accepted and it would have seemed to others to be no more than a chance encounter between a teacher and her pupil. But she was saying we had better not be seen together. She was letting me know what her feelings were.

We fell silent. She was impassive. She may have been waiting for me to leave, or she may have been inviting me to move closer. I did not have the courage to test her. I began to back away.

"Donald." Her voice was so subdued it seemed to draw greater darkness into the alcove and I moved with the shadows towards her. Just before our lips met she closed her eyes. She was so soft to the touch I could not tell if she was withdrawing or surrendering. But she did not repulse me.

The book she clasped was between us. Gently, I began to release it from her hands.

"No," she murmured, but at the same time she let her head fall back and that meant I could kiss her throat. She shuddered. "Not here," and she began to push me away until we were separated by the hands that held the book. "You do terrible things to me, Donald."

"Why don't we go somewhere else?"

She ignored that. "Don't you want to see what I found on the shelves?" she asked.

"No."

It was then that she raised her eyes to mine, taunting my eagerness. "You must wait. Let me show you the book."

She made me look at it. It was an Oscar Bullimore. "You didn't get that here," I said. I knew the shelves.

"Tucked away at the back."

"Oh no, it wasn't."

She put her face to mine and whispered into my mouth, "Oh yes, it was."

After a while I muttered, "I believe you."

She leant into me, her breath tickling my lips. "And when you get it signed for me there will be more of this." What she did next was unbearable. Her coat was apart and she pressed herself against me with such an insidious softness that all my control went and I thrust myself against her. "Donald!" She was half-amused. "You are far too keen – and I'm not one of your secretive contacts ... like Hazel Elliott of Barton Overhill."

Hazel again. "Contacts?" It was easy to sound puzzled. "And what's all this about Hazel Elliott?"

"I thought all you reporters had contacts for picking up gossip. Isn't that what Hazel provides – all the news of Barton Overhill?"

She was smiling, and I played along with her. "Oh, yes, Barton Overhill is full of secrets."

"Such as?"

She seemed serious, but my mind was blank. I raised my eyebrows and looked vague. "Nothing to report, Miss Cole. Nothing at all."

Her eyes searched my face as if testing the truth of what I was saying, and then she suddenly put a hand over my mouth. "Hush! There's someone on the stairs."

We listened. Nothing. But now she had put distance between us. And again that teasing smile.

"No more … not until you get Oscar's signature for me."

"But that will take ages – it'll have to go in the post."

"Then you'll have to wait."

"And so will you."

"But that is one thing I am able to do." She was almost the teacher once more. She pushed me backwards until we had moved out of the alcove. "Poor Donald, you look so crestfallen."

"Give me the book." I took it from her.

"You may bring it to me," she promised, "when you get it back."

"Tomorrow," I said.

She laughed at that.

"I mean it. I'll find a way."

She raised her eyebrows. "My word," she said primly, "you *are* keen."

Keen on what? She knew and I knew. It was the most provocative thing she had said. But I had to leave her. "Tomorrow morning," I said.

11

It was a night that put its claws into me from the start. I did not enjoy having to cycle all the way to town through the cut of the freezing air to play second fiddle to Jeremy Pyne. He had not had enough trust in me to tell me anything about the story that so interested him. To hell with you, Jeremy, I said as I stowed my bike in the works and became one of the few night wanderers drifting across the darkened market place. And when I had made my way down the sloping street to the river I was in no mood to admire the patchy mist, silvered by the moon, that lay on the water and spread over the yard of The Case is Altered.

One advantage of my mood was that, even though this was the first time I had been here alone,

I was careless about the pub's murky reputation, and the rattle of the latch that broke the silence as I entered did not worry me. Besides, according to Jeremy, it was the only serious pub in town; darts, beer from the barrel, no fruit machines and no music. And not much light, either. The short stone corridor inside the door was lit only by what escaped from the gloaming in the bar. No heads turned my way as I entered, but eyes move silently, and watching makes no sound. It was through a sea of looking that I approached the bar.

The landlord, captain of this dim ship, uttered no word, but by a lift of the chin gave me permission to speak.

"Pint." I was not going to grovel. "Bitter."

"Mild." The voice behind me brought me sharply round. "You drink with me, you drink mild." Jeremy put his own glass on the counter. "Same again for me, Norman."

Keeping his eye on the landlord pulling our drinks, he said, "I thought for one horrible moment you were going to ask for lager. Norman would have thrown you out – I hope."

The bar counter had more smile potential than Norman's face, but as we made our way to a table by the fire Jeremy said, "You're OK here, Don. He's taken to you in a big way."

That was nice to know. "I'd trust him with my

life," I said. "To take it." I glanced around the room. There was a lot of conspicuous muscle.

"You don't have to worry about this lot," said Jeremy. "Don't look 'em in the eye, that's all."

"No problem." I studied the flames of the meagre fire in the grate. "Why am I here?"

"Body parts." He spoke very softly, also looking into the fire.

"Whose body parts?"

"Anyone's body parts. This is where they are sold."

That was the trouble with working with a drunk like Jeremy; his sense of humour.

"Eyes in jars." I glanced at the bar. The big jar was topped up with pickled eggs. "Doesn't look as if they've done much trade tonight."

He did not take his gaze from the fire. "I saw it," he said quietly. "Just the one eye in a small jar. It was wrapped up, but the bag split. I was never meant to see."

There was not the hint of a smile on his face. He believed he had seen it. All I could think of was to play along with his hallucination; perhaps I could shake him out of it. "Who sells them?" I asked, and had to laugh as I said it.

"He isn't here yet." He bent forward as if to study the table top, but really to get his head closer to mine. "And for God's sake, Donald, keep your voice down. Nobody knows about it but us – not even Norman."

His fingertip was making patterns with a spilled drop of beer as he concentrated on it like a kid guilty of some sin. He was pale-faced and narrow-shouldered, no match for anyone in this room, but this was the company he preferred.

"No wonder you didn't tell Freddie about this," I said. "He'd never believe you." I was crediting Freddie with my own thoughts. Jeremy Pyne had lost touch with the real world.

Without raising his head he looked sideways at me. "You mean I'd never get the story past him? Too speculative, too dangerous?" There was the faintest smile on his face. "Don't worry, Chiefie won't get a sniff of it. This one goes straight to the nationals."

So now I knew what was driving him. He wanted to resume his old contacts with the nationals and escape the *Brackenridge Courier*. And he was using me as his accomplice.

He had read my thoughts. "They'll go for it," he said. "It'll be goodbye Chiefie, for ever."

"But body parts, Jeremy. Who gets them, and how?"

"That's the easy bit. Where's the obvious place to go?"

If this was serious I didn't want anything to do with it. I let my disgust show. "An undertaker?"

"Easier than that."

"Not a surgeon." Freddie had made me do hospital calls, and it was no crime centre.

"Not a surgeon." He shook his head but kept his eyes on me.

"A nurse?"

"Not a nurse."

I was about to ask him outright when his knee nudged mine under the table. "Don't look up whatever you do."

Jeremy drank. I drank. "Why?" I murmured.

"Because he's just come in." There was satisfaction in his voice as if he had had his doubts until this moment. "And he's brought it with him!"

I didn't ask, and I didn't look. For the first time my mind shifted into sickening possibilities.

Jeremy had brought his glass close to his face as if he was afraid of lip-readers. "Big guy at the bar with his back to us. Hospital porter."

Hospital porter. The words swung shut like a heavy door. I was trapped. His job was to go to the incinerator with whatever the surgeons had…

"Carrier bag," said Jeremy. "At his feet. That's it!"

I waited until Jeremy had looked round the room. When he nodded I glanced at the bar. The man was large and made more massive by the bulk of his windcheater. Christmas was coming and he was outlined in the glimmer of ancient fairy lights over the bar. It was a nice touch at that moment.

"A plastic bag." There was satisfaction in Jeremy's voice. "It has to be."

"Why?"

"Plastic is waterproof. No drips."

For a moment or two I did not grasp his meaning. Then I did. The bag, resting on the floor, was softly swollen at its base as if what it contained was moist, but nothing oozed.

"I've got to know what's in it." Jeremy was looking at me as if he expected me to tap the windcheater on the shoulder and ask.

I shook my head. "You do it."

A door opened and footsteps sounded on the flagstones of the corridor. The man at the bar turned his head.

"Now!" Jeremy was on his feet. "Come with me. Quick – and do whatever you have to."

I had no choice. I was looking at his back as he headed for the bar, taking off his coat at the same time. As if by accident his elbow caught the man at the bar. It was so blatantly deliberate that I winced and held back.

"I beg your pardon, friend." He had his hand on the porter's shoulder. "Hot in here." His coat dangled over the bag while he directed the man's attention away from it. "Let me buy you a drink."

The porter was not going to be fooled. He was trying to shrug the hand from his shoulder, frowning. "I'm on my way out," he grunted.

"I'm sorry to hear that." Jeremy's imitation of a drunk was not bad; he was drawing on experience.

"I jogged your elbow, friend – and I'd like to make up for it. One for the road… Just one little drink to say sorry."

Under cover of his dangling coat he had pushed the bag to one side with his foot. As he spoke he shot a glance at me with urgency in his eyes. It was now or never. I stepped close.

"Your coat's all over the place, Jeremy," I said, and tugged at it and stooped as I did so.

The plastic bagged gaped, but not enough to show anything inside. I put my hand to it. It was too dark down here to see anything. I must reach inside and feel … just one touch and away. The plastic was cold on my wrist. What lay inside was soft and wrapped in cloth. It was cylindrical. I felt swiftly along its length with eyes in my fingertips. Soft but firm and, as my fingers pressed gently at its end, it was soggily damp.

"I don't want a bloody drink!" The porter's voice was an angry growl, but he was holding it down, not wanting to attract attention. "Piss off!"

I had failed. I had no idea what was in the package, but as I was withdrawing my hand my fingers brushed its other end. It was the briefest contact, no more than a butterfly touch, but my fingers saw what they saw, and I jerked away with such revulsion that I pulled Jeremy with me and away from the porter.

"Sorry." I was apologizing to the scowl that was turned on me. I pulled Jeremy further back. "He's had enough. I'll get him home."

"You better bloody do that."

We backed off. The porter lost all interest in us and reached down to pick up the bag.

"Time to go, Jeremy." He came with me towards our table where my drink was unfinished.

"Did you see?" He swayed closer like a drunk, mumbling. "What is it?"

My attention was on the porter, and when I spoke I knew my words were inaudible. But the porter seemed no longer aware of either of us. A young woman had come in from the corridor.

"What did you say?" Jeremy's head was close to mine.

"It's an arm." My tongue was too thick to speak properly. "It's a human arm."

"You saw it?"

I shook my head. The girl seemed to be asking for change or seeking directions and the porter was offering help.

"Then how do you know it was an arm?" Jeremy's whisper was too loud, but the porter and the girl were moving away. "How do you know!"

"Because I felt…" I could not tell him how I had felt the scratch of the cold fingernails that had worked their way out of the wrapping. "It had fingers…" My voice faded. The girl. She had glanced briefly over her shoulder. I recognized her pale face.

"And…?" Jeremy was trying to shake it out of me. He was too insistent, and I raised my hand to free myself. As I did so his face changed. "Oh, my god!" he breathed.

The girl had turned away and the porter was following her out of the bar. "It's her," I said. "The one in the market place when—"

He did not hear me. He was clutching my wrist. "Your hand!" he said. "Look at your hand!"

"No, Jeremy." I tried to shake him off. "Listen!" But then I saw my fingers. They were mottled, patchy with black-red sticky blood.

I had touched a severed arm. We both knew it. But the porter had gone out with the girl, and I had to make Jeremy listen. We were still talking urgently, crouched over the table, when the door opened once again and the hospital porter returned. He was no longer carrying the bag.

"She has it!" Jeremy, cold sober, forced me to sit. "I've got to follow her. You stay here. One of us has to keep watch." I tried to rise but he made me keep my place. "I'm relying on you, Don," he said. There seemed no point in keeping watch on the porter any longer, but I did not protest. I let Jeremy go.

My glass was empty. I could not keep up the pretence of drinking, and the porter was leaning against the bar once more as if he was prepared to make a night of it. At any moment he would glance in my direction and I could not trust myself to seem innocent. I had to buy a drink. I was about to reach into my pocket for money when I saw my smeared hand. Disgust made me clench my fist and close my eyes. I groaned and someone laughed.

Very slowly I opened my eyes. The laugh came again from a table in the corner. Two men sat there. "We seen what you done." The one who had laughed got to his feet. He was an old man, the sort who watches and misses nothing, and he came out from behind his table and began to shuffle across the floor. I drew back in my seat, prepared for him to confront me, but he ignored me and headed for the bar. His words were for the hospital porter.

"Looked a bit heavy, that bag," he said. "Was it just one, or did you let her have a couple?"

"Just the one." The porter kept his voice low, not wanting to answer.

"I could do with a couple meself," said the man.

"Can't promise." The porter did not want to have anything to do with him, but the old man would not be shaken off.

"You get 'em, I'll have 'em. No questions asked."

The porter grunted and emptied his glass.

"Christmas is comin'," the old man said. "Don't forget."

By this time the porter was leaving but the old

man continued to talk to the barman. "You can keep your bloody turkeys," he said. "There ain't nothin' to beat a brace of pheasants on Christmas day."

And then I knew. It had been a bird's claw that had scratched my hand, and it was too late to do anything about it. Jeremy was out of reach, and tomorrow we would look foolish. I went out to wash pheasant blood from my fingers.

In the inn yard the icy mist lay waist-high but it was no longer a stage for mystery or fear. The night was empty of threat and even the car that lingered by the entrance, lightless but with its motor purring almost silently, meant nothing. A man was silhouetted against it, leaning down, talking to the driver. It was several seconds before I realized that the dark figure was the hospital porter and that the car, glimmering whitely through the mist, had police markings.

The policeman and the poacher. But the poacher was not at all troubled to be talking to the law, and there was nothing in his attitude to suggest he was being questioned. He was doing all the talking. I couldn't hear a word, but as he straightened he pointed into the road as if giving a direction. He stood back as the car's headlights stabbed suddenly into the mist and it moved out into the road and gathered speed.

12

A kind of carelessness comes over me every time a crisis ends. Jeremy's story had ended in fiasco, and now he was chasing a girl who had nothing more incriminating than a dead pheasant in the boot of her car. And I had been left to spy on a man who may have been a poacher but was friendly enough with the law to chat comfortably with a cop. Big deal.

Every detail of what had been happening to me had an explanation. And even when I tried to link them all together the connections seemed so thin that my brain creaked and refused to work at it any further. Perhaps I didn't want to know. Perhaps all I wanted to think about were pleasant things. Christmas was coming.

So when I got home that night I lied to Oscar Bullimore because it suited me. I needn't have done so, but I did. What, me worry? And my mother helped me without knowing it.

I gave him the book that Beatrice Cole wanted him to sign, and I made him a promise I had no intention of keeping. Authors are easy to understand. Until they pick up one of their own volumes in a second-hand bookshop and find it is one they inscribed for an admirer who promptly unloaded it, they all click up a little notch of self-esteem every time they sign. None were more greedy for clicks than Oscar, but this time when I put the book in front of him he hesitated. My mother saw it and said, "Is it for someone you don't like, Oscar?"

"I do not even know the lady, Madam." He was in his haughty mode, and this amused her even more.

"A lady?" She raised her eyebrows. "I've never known you disappoint one of your groupies."

"You alarm me!" A shudder rippled his plump cheeks. "*Groupies*, as you call them, are precisely what I have come here to avoid."

His true fears were a secret between him and me, and at that moment I would have gladly exposed them for the nonsense they were, but I played along with his story and said I would delay handing the book over without revealing his whereabouts. "I'll wait a couple of days before I give it to her." That was the lie. "I'll say I've had to post it to you – so that way she'll never guess you are here."

He beamed at my mother. "You must be proud of this young man, Joyce, my dear. He does all he can to protect a poor, querulous old man."

"Don't pile it on, Oscar; he's no angel." She turned to me. "So who is this admirer?"

There was no point in hiding it. "Miss Cole," I said briefly, as if it was a matter of no importance.

My mother, being one herself, knew every teacher in town. "Beatrice Cole," she said, her interest suddenly kindling. She gave Oscar a look full of meaning. "You'll like *her*, Oscar. All the sixth form boys have a crush on her, as Donald will tell you."

"Leave me out of it." I was piqued and had to struggle to disguise it. "She's just a teacher."

"My son may be young enough to be immune to her charms, Oscar, but she really does appeal to the mature man. You won't be sorry when you meet her."

"No!" I spoke so sharply I surprised her. I covered up. "You don't want to meet her, Oscar, do you? That's the whole point of it."

He sighed, and my mother smiled wickedly. "Sorry, Oscar."

"Your son is right, Mrs Jim." He uncapped his fountain pen. "So I must just pen a few words to the fair Miss Cole and—"

"Dark Miss Cole," she said.

He began writing in the book, murmuring as he did so: *"For my own Dark Lady, hoping that our paths will cross before too long."* His signature filled the rest of the page.

I took the book. "I promise she won't see it for several days," I said. Next morning I went to give it to her.

I was early. The antique dealer's rooms on the ground floor were still in darkness, but a cleaner or someone had left the outer door unlocked and I did not have to ring the bell. No one in the other flats need know she had a visitor and I was glad of it. I trod softly. It was as though I was climbing to her bedroom. Perhaps she was still asleep, and I visualized her waking and coming drowsily to open the door to me. The entire building conspired to make it possible. It was so empty of sound that furtiveness was forced on me and I floated upwards like a ghost with only the sound of my breathing to betray me.

I was ascending the last flight to her landing when I became aware I was not alone in the stairwell. A whisper came to me from above. It was a rustle as soft as silk, such as the hem of a nightdress might make as it brushed the carpet. And then I knew why the door was open, and my heartbeat deepened. She had been downstairs to collect her mail and had seen me as I turned the corner into the road. She had left it open and was waiting for me.

She would be listening, but I had been so secretive I might startle her. I began to climb carelessly so that she would hear me, but the whole building, which had colluded in my silence, refused to respond to my new wishes and, no matter how heavily I trod, my footsteps were muffled by the carpet. Was I to cough like a butler in a play ... or whistle? I was on the point of clearing my throat when my eyes came level with the landing.

Two people were talking, their voices mingling so softly I had taken the sound for the rustle of silk. I heard two but I could see only one. I saw his blue shirt and dark trousers as he stood just outside her door. And I could see his black shoes with their thick soles. At the far end of the rosy corridor a policeman was talking to Beatrice Cole.

I remained where I was, caught at the bend of the stairs. I had a reason for being there, but not even the book in my hand would have allowed me to climb the last few steps. I was an interloper. She had handed him his coat, and as he tilted his head I recognized him. That made it worse. Constable Martin Rose was young, slab-faced and as hard as marble. Although we made daily calls to the police station none of us, not even Freddie, had ever got to know him well, so we simply referred to him as The Constable and wrote him off as a source of information. He did not like reporters.

I strained my ears to hear what they were saying, but they spoke too softly. I was spying, and at any moment he would turn round and see me. I retreated, treading carefully, unable to run. I reached the floor below before I heard him following. His tread on the stairs creaked darkly, full of authority. He was certain to catch sight of me in the hall below, hurrying to get away unseen. I could already hear the shout, and then the questions.

At the foot of the stairs I turned sharply, ignoring the front door, seeking a way out at the back. After a few paces there was a door. It was locked. I pressed myself against it, shrinking into a corner. Now I was truly in hiding, and the law had me trapped. My only chance was that it was too early for lights to be on and I was in shadow.

I heard his bulky tread as he came down, and the bull's breath in his nostrils. His footsteps stopped. Only a thief would hide like this. My story was too thin for belief. I shut my eyes to become invisible and, as I squeezed them tight, the outer door slammed shut. He was gone.

As gradually as a snail coming out of its shell I expanded, and the return of courage warmed me. I still clutched Oscar's book and I had yet to deliver it. It was my passport to Beatrice Cole.

I climbed the stairs almost as quietly as before.

Thoughts of the constable were left below and had completely vanished by the time I knocked on her door. The only hint that she was not long out of bed was that she was preoccupied with doing up the top button of her dress as the door swung open. She did not even glance up as she stood back for me to enter. "What did you forget?" she asked.

"No. I remembered." I was smiling. "You didn't really think I'd forget, did you?"

She was startled. Her head jerked.

"I remembered," I repeated, and I held out the book.

Her eyes were darting over my face as if she failed to recognize me.

"It's me," I said, but she remained blank and I spoke clumsily. "I'm far too early. But I managed to get the book signed as I promised. Oscar Bullimore's book." At last she took it. "I know you didn't expect to get it so soon."

"Didn't I?"

"I told you we had to rely on the post," I reminded her. "I made a special effort."

"Did you?"

"I wanted you to have it before Christmas." I kept my eyes on her, willing her to comprehend the mysteriously special effort I had made on her behalf, and at last she seemed to understand.

"You saw him?"

I nodded.

"Even though he is in London?"

I let her read my face, and merely said, "I got Mr Bullimore to sign it."

"Thank you." She did not even glance at it, and my smugness faded. Nevertheless she seemed satisfied. "That was good of you," she said. There was no warmth in her voice.

"I'm glad you're pleased," I said. The meaningless words were building up, and the policeman had returned to my mind. Had he brought her bad news? I could not mention him without revealing that I had been lurking on the stairs, and she would not now be closing the door on me unless something was troubling her. I suddenly asked, "Is your car all right?" It was an inspiration; a brilliant stroke.

"What do you mean?" She frowned.

"I saw a policeman outside looking at it." I had practically asked her about him without revealing where I had been.

"What did he do?"

"He looked at it." That was lame, and it got lamer. "Then he walked away."

"Then there couldn't have been anything wrong," she said. "I've had no call from any policeman this morning."

She closed the door. The light from the rose-coloured window was no longer warm; the landing was hideously cold.

13

Freddie, with his tiny stub of a pencil, was writing tiny initials in the diary when I got in. He was alone in the reporters' room.

"Our mutual friend has gone missing." He did not look up, and I did not reply.

"Any ideas?" His words were directed at the diary.

"About what?" I spoke to the crown of his drab hat. Beatrice Cole had put vinegar in my voice, and my tone brought his head up. The yellow light made him grubby and small, but his bright beady eyes dared me to challenge him.

"I was referring to our mutual friend," he repeated.

"You mean Jeremy?"

"Where is he?"

"I've no idea."

He saw he was getting nowhere, and he relented a fraction. He tried to buy me.

"Christmas is coming." He pointed to a couple of six-packs of lager stacked on his desk. "They come with season's greetings from the manager of the Bell Hotel," he said. "Good of him to think of us."

"The usual bribery." I quoted Jeremy at him. "A couple of pints at Christmas and they expect favours for the rest of the year."

His lips were suddenly pinched and his face was mean. "I was intending to offer you our friend's share."

"Lager?" I said. "Jeremy doesn't touch it. Nor do I." Which was a lie but intended to annoy.

He was instantly busy with the diary. "Mr Pyne has not deigned to be with us," he said, heavily underscoring each word by putting pressure on his pencil stub, "so I am afraid you will have to undertake his assignments."

Which was why, my heart free of all attachments, I found myself alone in the firm's van, driving out to do a story about a landlord who had erected a Father Christmas and all his reindeers along the roof-ridge of his pub.

A hard winter had sealed the countryside and frosted the verges, and although the heavy clouds slumped low they were thrifty with snow so that only a few flakes danced in my wake. There would not be the Christmas-card scene for the front page that Freddie was hoping for, so the old Speed Graphic on the seat beside me would get only the plainest of shots of the Jolly Farmer at Barton Overhill. Not that it mattered. The *Courier* had never had a true photographer, and all our Speed Graphic plates were developed by the photographer on the market place who had a talent for making a plain picture even plainer, so a distant shot of the landlord standing outside his pub with Santa overhead would have to do. Not that I cared.

Stone barns, built long before cars, jutted into the road at awkward angles as I drove down into the village, which meant that I came across the Jolly Farmer unexpectedly and then had to stand with one foot almost in a frozen stream before I could get it all in my view-finder.

"That's some camera you got there, reporter," said the landlord. "How much do you want for it?"

"It's an antique," I said. "It prints on stained glass."

"Well, you better use this," and he handed me his Polaroid.

I got a couple of shots good enough to please Freddie, and for half an hour we sat in front of the fire in the bar. All I wanted was a caption but I got enough gossip to fill a page; none of it usable. It kept my mind off the humiliation of Beatrice Cole, however, but at last I had to go.

"Too early to offer you a drink," he said. Another humiliation; his shrewd eyes had been sizing me up and he had decided I was not seasoned enough for alcohol before nightfall. "But I tell you what, young feller, next time you're out this way you can have lunch on the house, you and your girlfriend."

"Haven't got one." None of his business. I stood up, searched my pockets for the van keys, and discovered I had left them in the ignition. Inexperience showed, and made him laugh.

"Don't worry, boy, you'll find a girl easy enough – plenty around here if you look."

"I didn't see any." The village had been deserted as I drove in.

"But they seen you." He was laughing at me again. "You'll be lucky to get away in one piece."

Which meant that I was less surprised than I may have been when I went out and saw there was a girl sitting in the passenger seat waiting for me. Hazel Elliott. She seemed unsure whether to smile or blurt out an explanation. When she saw my face she did neither. She looked first of all afraid, and then ashamed. And I did not know how to behave towards a girl I'd found gazing into her lap as if it wouldn't take much to make her cry. I know it's a weapon they have, and it works with me all the time, but Hazel Elliott was not faking. She was a girl in distress.

"I'd forgotten you lived here," I said.

"I can't help it."

What did that mean? She spoke so softly it couldn't have been a joke, so did she mean something had happened to force her into the passenger seat or, worse still, was it a passion for me she could not resist? No, I wasn't as vain as that.

I sat behind the wheel and closed the door. The key was where I had left it, in the ignition, but I did not know whether to switch on. "Can I take you somewhere?" I asked.

"Donald." She turned towards me too swiftly, and the word had come out so suddenly that she had startled herself. Our shoulders touched, and our faces were so close that the gap that would normally have separated us had been broken. The bubbles of space we lived in had joined. Our faces were too close, and it was an accident that made my lips brush hers. It wasn't a kiss. Even now, looking back at it, it wasn't a kiss. It was only the slightest touch, our eyes remained open, and a moment later I sat back as if nothing had happened.

We ignored it. It was too trivial a thing to mention. She seemed to want to say something, but I did not want to hear. I switched on and drove out of the inn yard.

We had driven half a mile before she told me why she had so daringly got into the van to wait for me. It was not that she was throwing herself at my head – nothing like that, but as she was speaking I could tell it was costing her an effort to disguise what she felt. I know I was vain, but I wanted her to be attracted to me. She was a girl, wasn't she?

"I don't want to cause you any trouble, Donald." She did not look at me. "I don't want you to think…" and her voice dropped away. We had kissed, almost kissed, but she would not let herself believe that I meant it. She sat with her hands in her lap prepared for any disappointment I would inflict.

I grunted, meaning no more than I understood what she was saying, but I saw her entwined fingers tighten. "Stop," she said. I had hurt her.

I pulled on to the verge. "I'll take you home."

"No. I've got something to tell you."

She managed at last to put aside what had happened between us. "Look over there." She pointed through the windscreen. The road ahead curved along the flank of the hill, rising towards the crest. There were trees and an occasional field gate but nothing remarkable. "No," she said, "further away, across the valley – the house. That's where Mr Slade lives."

A stream scrawled an unsteady line across the

valley floor, and the house stood alongside it within a clump of trees.

"Yesterday," she said, "I tried to get there. It's got its own road – between those hedges, see?" I could just make out what seemed to be a double row of hedges leading down to the trees. "It's no more than a track," she said, "but it's the only way to get there."

"Why did you go?"

I saw dishonesty in her face for the first time. Her eyes looked sidelong at me and a patch of colour appeared on her cheeks. "I was curious," she said. "After that thing we saw in the market place."

The finger. But that alone would not have made her take risks. "You wanted to help me," I said.

The colour heightened in her face. "You saw it. We both saw it." It had become real. We both knew that what we had seen was a real finger. All my wishes to make it something else dissolved and vanished.

"But what did you think you were going to do at the house down there?" I asked. "What were you going to say to him?"

"I wasn't going to meet him. I was just going to look."

It may have seemed fierce the way I turned towards her then, but my mind was racing through what must have happened. "You didn't go there yesterday," I said. "You went there last night. After dark. By yourself."

She could not hold my gaze, and her eyes dropped as she nodded. There had to be more. I waited.

"I didn't get there." She raised her eyes. "I had a torch ... but I didn't dare switch it on because the people in the house might have seen, so just before I got down to the stream something made me stumble."

"*Made* you stumble?"

"It seemed like it. A bit of grass or something twisted around my ankle and I fell down. I tried to kick it off as I got up, but it clung, and as I dragged my foot away it came with it ... and it wasn't like grass at all ... it was *heavy*!" She was drawing her feet up as she spoke, and she wasn't in the van with me any longer. "It was heavy and it wouldn't go. I hit it." She stabbed as if her hand still held the torch. "It clung on! And I yelled and kicked and kicked until I flung it off." Her mouth and eyes were wide as the terror returned. "It hit the ground and lay there. It was white. Something white."

I had to know what it was. "You had a torch," I said.

"I couldn't make it work. I broke it. And then –" her eyes slid away as if she still gazed down at what lay at her feet – "and then it moved. It started to crawl!"

"Towards you?" I held out my hand and it was what she needed. She reached out and clung to it.

"I don't know. It seemed to be searching, looking for me. I ran, Donald. I ran away."

I glimpsed something move in my wing-mirror. A car was coming and the road was narrow. I wasn't sure it could get by so I waited. The car slowed, pulled closer to the hedge on the offside, and as it drew level I turned towards it. The driver was concentrating on the hedge that was brushing the side of the car. It was Beatrice Cole. She did not once look in my direction, and I watched her out of sight around a bend in the road.

Seconds later we saw the top of Beatrice Cole's car as it made its way between the hedges of the track down to the house at the bottom of the valley.

14

My eyes were on Beatrice Cole's car disappearing into the lane, but the picture in my mind was of something else. The roof of her car dwindled between the hedges, but I was seeing myself as I tapped at the door of her flat that morning. I had been sure of myself, certain of charming her … until she had opened the door. Her expression had told me what she saw: a tiresome young fool, as raw as a worm.

And that was what Hazel Elliott could also see.

"I'll take you home." I heard my voice say the words calmly enough, but my foot kicked a frenzy into the old van's engine, and my disgust with myself sent us rocking and screeching into the road and almost killed us. I side-swiped a bank, veered off it and lurched across the road to a steep drop on the other side. I trod on the brakes, chewed deep furrows into the verge and pulled up with a heave that pitched us both forward.

In the middle of the lurch Hazel cried out. This put me in a temper that had me reversing back into the road so carelessly that I terrified her again. I was a bully boy, and I suddenly saw it. I slowed down. "I don't know exactly where you live," I said.

"Anywhere in the village will do."

I glanced at her. She looked very cold. Her cheeks were pale. She could not know what had angered me, and I could not tell her.

I slowed again when we came to the village but would not stop until she had directed me to a lane behind the inn. If this was where she lived it would have been easy for her to have seen the van in the inn yard.

"I'm sorry about that bit of a skid back there," I said.

"That's all right." Her voice was very quiet.

We pulled up. Her hand went to the door handle but rested there limply.

"I was angry," I said.

She paused before she replied. "Miss Cole can't be doing anything bad," she said. So she had linked the way I had behaved with catching sight of Beatrice Cole. "She can't be doing anything wrong – everyone likes her."

"Not everyone."

"She's very pretty."

I made no answer. I was staring ahead at the haphazard row of stone cottages in the lane. A man came out of one and looked towards us.

"What I mean is – " Hazel began to talk rapidly – "just because she's nice to look at doesn't mean anything. She may be horrible, for anything I know, but I still don't think she can be mixed up in something."

"Mixed up in what?" In spite of everything, I found myself still defending Beatrice Cole.

"You know what I'm talking about!" Her voice was sharp enough to bring my head around, but her attention was not on me any longer. The man from the cottage was coming towards us. "It's my father!" She was in a panic of shyness and she tugged at the door handle, wanting to get out so that I should not have to meet him. "It won't open!" She was banging at the door ineffectively and there was nothing for it but that I had to go round and tug it from outside.

Her father came closer. "Door's jammed," I said.

"So I see." He had the all-weather face of a countryman, his eyes well protected by wrinkles. He seemed amused to see his daughter trapped behind glass. "How about leaving her there? Save us all a lot of trouble."

I managed to grin. It was very odd to think of

Hazel as truly troublesome. "Don't you want her?" I asked.

"Do you?" His wrinkles deepened. He had me in a corner and knew it.

I shrugged. But this was no compliment to his daughter and I immediately felt bad about it. "You know what I mean," I said.

"Maybe I do, maybe I don't. It's just to be hoped *she* knows." He was chuckling as, to escape losing more ground, I heaved at the handle. There was mud on the side of the van where it had left the road, and the branch of a bush had wedged itself under the door. Her father worked it free and the door opened.

"I hit a bank," I admitted.

"There was a car coming the other way, Dad," Hazel said. "He couldn't help it."

Her eyes rested on mine. There was a boldness in her I had not seen. She was doing more than protect me from her father's ridicule; she was telling me that what we had been talking about was a secret between us.

I had to have lunch there. Hazel's mother had seen us working on the van and she insisted on setting another place at the kitchen table. She was a contrast to her husband, plump where he was thin, and she had her own way of making me feel at home. "You must be that young reporter we've been hearing so much about," she said.

"No doubt about it; he's the one," said her husband, knowing very well what he was doing. It was only then that Mrs Elliott noticed that Hazel was embarrassed, and she turned on him.

"Take off that stupid cap," she ordered. "And sit down."

"Watch out, boy," he said as he hung his cap behind the door, "no matter what they look like they always get the better of you in the end."

"Pay him no heed." Mrs Elliott turned to me. "He talks a lot of old squit." But then she blundered into another subject I would rather had not been mentioned. Oscar Bullimore. "I read your piece about him in the paper," she said. "It must be very interesting getting to know people like that."

"He's just like anyone else," I told her. "Or that's what Oscar says."

"Drinks a bit by the look of him," said Mr Elliott.

"You've got no right to say that about someone's friend!" His wife was indignant. "I'm sure Mr Bullimore is very sober."

"Now and again." I got a laugh from Hazel's father.

"Well, he's a very modest man, that I do know," said Mrs Elliott. "Hazel was telling me he doesn't want anyone to know where he is – isn't that right?"

We all looked at Hazel. I had told her nothing. "I just guessed," she said. "It must have been the way you wrote it; it made me think he didn't want anyone to know."

I made things easier for her. "He doesn't."

"Well where is he?" It was her father again. "I should think you know."

I was looking at Hazel as I opened my mouth to speak, but suddenly I stopped. Only one other person had asked me that question.

"You don't have to say anything, boy." Hazel's father made me realize my mouth was still open. "You reporters have to keep your secrets, I don't doubt."

"No, it's not that, Mr Elliott." I hesitated, not knowing what to say to be tactful and still keep Oscar's secret.

"Don't you worry, Donald." He was letting me off the hook; it was the first time he had used my name. "There's no need to say another word."

But the damage had been done. "I did make a promise," I admitted, and as I spoke my mind slid over a precipice. I had already betrayed Oscar, and I suddenly saw how it had happened. Beatrice Cole had been too clever for me. She had wheedled it out of me when she had asked for Oscar's signature. I had returned the book so swiftly it was obvious that I saw him every day. And when I eventually turned up with the book itself she had no need of it; she had already found out what she wanted to know. But why was it so important to know where Oscar was? There was only one reason. I groaned and just managed to turn it into a sigh. "I've just remembered," I said. "I've got to get back to the office."

It was obvious that I was trying to get away. Mrs Elliott looked anxiously at her daughter, and so did I. I had to talk to Hazel.

"We are short-handed at the *Courier*," I said. "Someone didn't turn up today." It was true, but it also gave me a chance to talk to Hazel alone. She went out to the van with me and I opened the passenger door. "Sit with me for a minute," I said, and saw her look anxiously towards the house. "I know what they'll think," I said. "They'll put me down as your boyfriend."

"I'm sorry," she said.

"I'm not." That surprised us both. Me in particular. But what really startled me was that it was no surprise at all. Somehow, deep inside, I had always known that she and I … shy Hazel Elliott and me… And now I had no time to think about it. Except that Beatrice Cole was always linking us together when she really had no motive for doing so. And then, sickeningly, my mind tilted and I saw what it meant. I had just seen Beatrice Cole heading for the house of Mr Slade. Something was happening there, and Beatrice Cole had been trying to discover from me if Hazel knew anything about it. She had never wanted me. I had been used.

"There's something I've got to know," I said. "Tell me about that man Slade. How long has he lived there?"

"A long time. Years. But he comes and goes and nobody really knows him."

"He has people visit him?"

"A few," she said, "but no one gets to know them. Everyone in the village says they are just snobbish, but…"

She was uncertain whether to go on, but I urged her and she said, "We were always afraid of that house when we were kids because someone said that a strange red man lived there."

"Red?"

"That's what they always said, but I know what it was because my father saw this 'red man' one day. It was only a sort of statue of a man – not a very good one because it looked very clumsy and wasn't bright red at all, just reddish and rather dull."

She saw my expression change. "What is it, Donald?"

"The terracotta coffin," I muttered. "The Black Dawn." I gripped her arm. "We've found them!"

So swiftly it was no more than a gabble I told her about L'Aube Noire and the Marquis de Terre Cuite, and Oscar's story … and Oscar's terror. And then I told her Oscar's secret. "Oscar Bullimore is living with us and I've got to get to him. He's in danger and won't answer the phone."

"But why?"

"He's afraid to answer the phone in case it's one of them and then they'll know where he is."

"So he's safe for the moment," said Hazel.

"Not now. Beatrice Cole is one of them — and she knows where he is because I've as good as told her!"

15

I had to get out of the van to open the jammed door for Hazel. She did not waste time questioning me about my betrayal of Oscar Bullimore, and she had seen Beatrice Cole heading for the house in the valley. "What will we do?" was all she wanted to know.

"Oscar first," I said. "I've got to get to him."

"What about your office? They'll want to know where you've been."

I thought of Freddie and his pencil stub. "Let them fret. I'll say I had an accident." Which was true. Mud and grass still clung to the door. Evidence.

She had left the house without a coat and was shivering. There was silence for a moment and we each looked away. There was danger but we did not know how it would come. Doubts came crawling in.

"You've got to let me know what happens," she said. Last night she had risked a lonely lane in the dark; now her eyes were absorbing me as if she feared to let me go. I swung myself up into the van as if I was straddling a horse.

Thirty miles to go and the clouds were already bringing twilight to the valleys. I stopped at the first phone box but my call went into nothingness. Oscar was letting it ring. I did not want the van to be seen in town so I threaded my way through the outskirts and found myself in the narrow road where Jeremy had a bed-sit. The outer door of the house was locked and no one answered the bell. His usual parking space in the road was empty. I thought of calling the office and asking to speak to him, but the blank space at the kerbside and the dark window of his room seemed to tell me it was a forlorn hope. Jeremy was somewhere else.

There was almost no traffic once I had left the town, and by the time I had turned into our lane and had crackled to a standstill on the frozen gravel, the only sound came from the breeze combing the bare hedges. The house was dark, but firelight flickered cheerfully in the room at the back where Oscar made himself comfortable. He had kept up his precautions and all was well.

I knocked at the back door but got no reply. He

would be asleep in his chair by the fire, and in order not to disturb him I unlocked the door and let myself in.

"Oscar – are you there?" I opened the door to the room quietly so as not to startle him. It was very cosy in the firelight, and I went over to where I could see him slumbering in his chair. "Wake up, Oscar. I've got something to tell you."

But there was no one there. I was speaking to a pile of cushions. I had entered without putting on the light, but now I stooped to the table lamp beside the chair and switched it on. The room was empty and I was straightening when my hand knocked over an envelope propped against the lamp. My name was on it in Oscar's flamboyant scrawl. I tore it open. The message inside was brief.

Donald – A note to put your mind at rest. A certain person called to see you this afternoon but chanced upon me instead, and I was recognized. She is an ardent reader of my work, so tonight I dine with a fair admirer (and one so discreet that she forbade me to leave this note, so I pen it in secret). My cover is blown but all is well!

Oscar Bullimore

She had got to him. His signature was a banner of triumph, but she had numbed him with her sting and would devour him from inside like a parasite.

My mind twisted into confusion. I went to the telephone. There was nothing else to help me. And then, grasping it, I did not know how to use it. The police? Even if the constable did not pick up the phone he would hear about it. Jeremy Pyne? He was unreachable. It had to be Hazel. I had started to dial her number when I heard a voice.

"Donald!" It was a small, thin sound and seemed to come from the handset. I put it to my ear. The tiny voice came again.

"Donald!"

It sounded far off. I pressed my ear to the phone.

"Donald!"

Not within the handset at all. I raised my head. My name was in the air, but it did not come from within the room. I put down the phone. The thread of sound drew me into the hall and I listened at the foot of the stairs. My name came again. From downstairs. At the back of the house. It came from outside. I opened the door and let the night in.

The bare, black hills kept their distance, looking down, and deep shadow covered the yard, the outhouses and the garden shed under the trees. Something was expecting me.

I hung back, listening but not moving. Then I heard a sound, but it was not my name. It was someone clearing his throat. It was a weak rattle that dragged on as if whoever was there was trying to speak but was too exhausted. I took half a pace back into the shelter of the house.

The voice gave a feeble cough … and I raised my hand to the torch that we kept hanging on the hat-pegs behind the door. I listened, but all was silent. I levelled the torch and switched it on. Its beam jabbed the night and instantly the voice responded.

"I'm over here, Donald."

"Where?" I swung the beam like a stick as if I would thrash the speaker out of existence.

"I am here."

The shed beneath the trees. I held the beam on it. "Come out." I kept my voice steady. "I want to see you."

The words that answered were hoarse and came slowly. "Is that what you really want, Donald?" Laughter gurgled into a painful cough, but when the voice resumed there was amusement in it that made it almost familiar. The words were spaced out. "Would you really like to see me, Donald?"

And then I knew. Jeremy. It was his voice, slower and thicker than I had ever heard it, but I was sure. "Jeremy. Where are you?"

And he laughed. He was hoaxing me. He had left me behind last night and he had not been seen all day. He, like me with the pheasant in the bag, had discovered that his lead on a good story had fallen flat, and now he was poking fun at me for seeing menace in places where there was none. I was laughing at my own fears when I went to the shed and opened the door.

And Jeremy was there. My torch beam fell on him sitting nonchalantly in one of the garden chairs we stored there. His head was half-turned away from me. It was typical of him. "You're a devil, Jeremy." I was relieved and slightly angry at the same time. "What the hell do you think you're playing at?"

"Nothing much, old son. Not any more." He did not bother to turn towards me. I stepped into the shed.

"You and me," I said, "we're both in Freddie's bad books. He'll skin us alive."

That made him laugh. "Is that a fact?" His lank black hair was slicked to one side and I doubted he could see me. His cheek in the torchlight was waxy pale.

"Jeremy…" I wanted him to turn my way. "Are you all right?"

"That's a matter of opinion, old boy." He gave a hacking rumble of a laugh. He did not stir.

"Jeremy." I lowered my voice and repeated his name as I went closer. My torch flickered over the limp hand, the sleeve of his coat, the neck of his jacket and, as I came round in front of him, the beam lit his face.

Half of it was there. The other half was missing;

hacked away. His ear had gone, one eye was a red socket, and very little remained of his mouth.

All my strength departed in one long shuddering moan that pushed me backwards to the wall. And there I stood, motionless. My hand that held the torch was wedged somehow against my ribs, and held steady so that the face was illuminated. It was the face of a corpse. Jeremy was dead. His corpse was in front of me, propped in a chair, and his head was half-skinned.

The overlapping cheek muscles twitched and writhed as the face laughed through clotted blood. "Enough, Donald?" it asked. "Have you seen enough?"

I flashed the beam from corner to corner. I was alone in the shed with Jeremy's corpse. "How?" I forced my dry throat to grate out the words. "Who is talking?"

"Me, of course. Jeremy. And another of your friends is due to join me this evening. Oscar Bullimore and I will soon be in the same condition. Isn't that nice?"

The torchlight glinted in Jeremy's dead eye, and for one ghastly moment his intelligence seemed to come to life and bore into me. He was telling me, merely by sitting there dead in my garden shed, that whoever was speaking through Jeremy's tortured mouth must not know what I knew. There was one question I must ask and in that instant I knew what it was but, before I had control of my breath, his corpse was speaking again.

"I have been sent to keep you quiet, Donald." The words were as ragged-edged as his torn mouth. "What you are witnessing at this moment will never be believed, but if you so much as breathe a word then you will know what fate awaits someone who is very fond of you. She will end up looking like me."

In the sudden jar of panic that hit me I blurted out the question. "Where is Oscar Bullimore?"

Whoever was speaking through Jeremy was bound to lie. I knew that, but my feverish brain, triggered by the glint in Jeremy's eye, also knew that the answer – whatever it was – would be my chance to mislead.

Jeremy's throat was congealing. His words were forced out. "Oscar Bullimore is already a hundred miles from here, far out of your reach."

Once more my torch caused a gleam in his dead eye, and I answered one lie with another. "He's been taken back to London," I said, and I let my head droop in despair.

And the corpse gave me an order. "Switch off that light and leave. Do nothing, and by morning I shall have gone."

I had to teach my feet to walk. Stumbling from time to time, I crossed the yard into the house, locked the door and crouched behind it. I could not control my shuddering as I pressed myself into the corner. My reaction was so violent that the door trembled with me, but I knew one thing for certain: Oscar was not in London. Oscar had fled from London, and I had let them believe I also thought the threat came from there. But Oscar was with the Black Dawn, and they were within reach of where I crouched in terror.

16

Crouching behind the door, I listened. It was hours before my parents were due home, but before long there would be visitors. They were coming for the corpse. Before morning, dead Jeremy had said. That meant they were occupied elsewhere … with Oscar. My heart was hammering and I could barely think, but I knew where they were taking him, and that they were ignorant of how much I knew.

I was gasping as I fought to control my thoughts, but suddenly I saw it all. The cunning of the members of the Black Dawn who years ago had hidden themselves in the valley of Barton Overhill; the trip they had taken to London to ensnare Oscar; and then their good fortune when they lost him only to find that the clue they needed was close to hand and that I was the link that would betray him.

And new panic came rushing into the dark house as I realized what I had to do. My ragged heartbeat raced my tattered breath and I clawed myself through the hall and out. I had the urge to run and hide and run again, but sense came from somewhere and slowed me down. I was stiff with fear as I jerked open the van door, climbed in and slammed it shut, and I had to clench my hands together to control their trembling and get the key into the ignition.

In the wrong gear I screamed into the lane without lights and howled down the road for half a mile before my joints unclamped and my brain unfroze enough to put me in charge of what I was doing.

I did not have the courage to stop on a country road, and once I was in town I had to avoid the police station, but I found a quiet street and drew up near a phone box. There was only one person I could call, but it was her father who answered, and when Hazel came to the phone I suddenly realized I could not pour out the horror I had been through.

"Can I see you?" It was all I trusted myself to say.

There was a pause. I could hear the television in the background. She was in the living room with her parents. "When?" she said quietly.

"Now. It has to be now."

She was whispering. "They'll want to know where I'm going."

"Tell them…" I tried to think of something but my mind refused. "Tell them…"

She heard what was in my voice and made up her mind. "The pub car park," she said. "Same place as this afternoon. Can you make it?"

I nodded, ridiculously, but she had guessed. "I'll think of something to tell them." She raised her voice. "I'll be there. Don't be long."

Driving out of town was difficult. I did not want to leave the lights behind and only by muttering to myself like a madman as I clung to the steering wheel did I manage to put the miles of dark road behind me. I came to the top of the hill and looked down into the valley. Her village showed only a few reluctant winks of light. It was not a place where anything happened at night, and I rode down into it bringing terror with me. She knew it before I said a word.

I did not see her as I stepped out of the van and, when I heard my name called from the shadows, I shrank back and was on the point of running until she came into the light.

"Tell me," was all she said.

I did so. Every detail, feeding the horror of it to her. "Jeremy's dead," I said. "But he talks."

Her face was perfect, as pale as a lily against the

gloom, but what she said was hideous. "That means they have his skin," she said, "and someone is wearing it."

"Parts of his head." I had to force myself to say it.

"Enough to make him talk."

"And hear and see," I said. We clung together as though the black tide in our brains was sweeping us away. Somewhere there was a mouth that wore the skin of Jeremy's tongue and lips and spoke through his corpse.

"Oscar Bullimore," I said. Anything to drive away the worst that was swamping us. "They've got him."

Hazel drew back slightly. "We need help."

I knew we did, but we would get none. Too much to explain. And no time. It was then that I kissed Hazel properly for the first time. I needed to. She was lovelier than anyone I had ever met, and I had to let her know that I surrendered to her. Once and for all. And even then she outdid me. She made the whole night giddy with longing. I trod fear underfoot and opened the door of the van.

The hill road was exposed but after a mile we found a gate into a field and took the van through and hid it behind a hedge. Cattle snorted somewhere nearby but were hidden in the darkness. We were not afraid of them, nor of anything; and we should have been.

I found a large torch in the glove compartment and gave it to Hazel. The battery was almost dead and it gave out no more than a gleam but it could serve as a weapon. For myself I took the largest spanner I could find in the tool kit. It was the best we could do.

She led the way. The valley, dark and empty, yawned to the sky, and the mouth of the lane was almost invisible when we came to it.

Last night something had caught at her ankle. "Where did it happen?" I whispered.

"Nearer the house. It came out of the bushes."

I went ahead, a pace at a time, keeping to the centre of the track. For every new bush or tree that loomed into sight a new stretch of darkness closed in behind. It was as if the house was sucking us towards itself, and we paused often to listen. We heard nothing. The grass was frozen to silence, nothing came scratching towards us, and after an age of creeping deeper and deeper into the valley the darkness ahead arranged itself into what could have been a rooftop and a wall with the black sockets of windows.

We went forward as noiselessly as breathing and then, almost before we knew it, the track widened into a forecourt across which the house was gazing at us. A car stood in its shadow.

We paused, heads together, about to mouth words, when the treetops high above us were suddenly startled into life. They were brilliantly floodlit. The light was as stark and bright as a shout in the night and made our heads jerk back but, as suddenly as it had appeared, the light vanished. Thumping seconds passed when again the light swept the treetops, and this time we saw where it came from. A car had turned off the hill road and was dipping into the track behind us.

It came fast. We flung ourselves face down in the long grass at the foot of the hedge an instant before the beam jostled over the track. Dust was still settling on us when I raised my head and saw the car swing to a stop sidelong to the house. It was white with a red and blue stripe along its side. No blue light had flashed, but the constable was in a hurry. His door slammed before the last gleam faded from the headlamps, and he was raising the boot-lid as the front door of the house opened and someone came out.

There were voices, but no words reached us. The constable needed help in lifting something from the boot, and the two of them were having trouble because it was either heavy or delicate. A third person came out with a flashlight and for some time all three were busy behind the car and out of sight.

I had half raised myself in order to crawl forward and get a better view when Hazel hauled suddenly at my elbow and brought me flat.

"No!" Her voice was in my ear. "Don't move!"

She was too cautious. The group behind the car were so occupied there was no risk in moving closer. I tried to prise her fingers from my arm but she gripped tighter.

Some limp weight sagged between the constable and one of his companions as they came from behind the car while the third person lit the ground in front of them. I could make out nothing until they climbed the steps to the door. Then the dim light from the corridor inside showed what they carried between them. It was Jeremy. I muttered his name between clenched teeth as I struggled not to shudder. The constable had been to fetch him.

Before turning to go indoors the figure with the flashlight swept its beam across the forecourt. The light touched the tops of the grass and paused directly over our heads. Hazel's fist tightened as if she wanted to tell me something, but I did not need to be told to be motionless. I saw her face. She was not looking at me, nor at the beam. Something away to the side held her gaze and horrified her. I moved my eyes and saw it. Three paces from us there was a gleam in the hedge. The beam had sought it out and held steady.

The gleam was an eye, but an eye without a head. It was a naked eye, lidless and forever staring, a human eye skewered on a stick and keeping watch on whatever approached the house.

17

We worked our way back, away from the eye.

"It can see," I said. I was speaking to keep another thought out of my mind. "There's someone in the house who sees what it sees." Looking through the eye, skewered there, in front of us. At that instant, the thought that I had pushed to the back of my mind rose to obliterate everything else. It was Jeremy's eye that glared into the night. Anger drove me now. Hatred and fury.

"Other things…" Hazel's whisper was unsteady. Last night something had clawed her ankle. "There could be other things." We were looking at each other but all our senses were on the darkness around us.

I grunted and bent my head closer to hers. "There's got to be another way in," I said. "They won't be watching the back." Perhaps, but we both knew it was our only choice. And at that moment we wavered. We could turn our backs and go for help. Jeremy was already dead. Nobody would blame us.

"Oscar Bullimore," she breathed. "He must be in there."

This time we had no choice. We went back up the track until we came to a low point in the hedge and pushed through. She had shaken off some of her fear. "We can run," she said. "Cattle run at night, so we won't set off any alarm."

And by running we would lessen the chance of lurking hands snatching at us. She went plunging down the hill with me following. They had Oscar; we were racing against time.

It was rough pasture, but we had night eyes and we leapt the tussocks as we flew downhill to the stream at the bottom. I was about to cross it when Hazel held me back. "We stay with it," she said. "It goes close to the house." She stepped into the water. "It's not deep. If we go slowly it will hide our sound."

Trees arching the stream made a winding tunnel and I could not see the water that rose to my knees and pulled at my legs with black fingers. I held on to Hazel's coat as she felt her way ahead, warning me of deeper spots where we waded slowly. We only made faster progress when our splashing merged with the rippling shadows.

We took breath, panting like animals. "We are close now," she muttered and pointed. The bank of the stream shelved up to a lawn. At the far side we could make out the house. Curtains were drawn, but there was light in one of the lower rooms.

We emptied our shoes of the icy water. The coldness no longer mattered and we had ceased to shiver. There was a lawn dotted with trees and we crossed it as silent as cats. In the shelter of the last tree we paused. Its bare branches reached out to touch the iron framework of an old conservatory built along the back of the house. The glass was grimed, but through it we could see French windows in the back wall of the house and another more solid door under which a chink of light showed. There would be too much danger if we tried to enter through the door, but the French windows were dark. They were our best chance, but first we had to cross the conservatory. I tried the iron handle of the conservatory door. It was locked. I rubbed the glass and put my face close.

"The key is on the other side," I whispered.

"How can we get it without making a noise?"

I was already taking off my windcheater. I had the wrench from the van. I put it inside the sleeve and wrapped the rest of the coat around it until it was well padded. She guessed what I was doing. The smallest pane was nearest the lock but nothing could prevent the sound of falling glass inside. She took off her own coat and spread it against the glass to muffle the sound even further. The silence within the house was our enemy, and the lawn at our backs was watching as I drew back the padded wrench and hit the glass. Nothing broke, but the rattle of the ironwork told the night that we were there.

We stood as still as the iron stanchions that held the roof and gazed across the stone floor inside. For a full minute we waited while the mist of our breathing hung in the air, but no footsteps sounded.

We both leant hard against the conservatory door to hold it still. I did not have the courage to fail a second time. I drew back the wrench and rammed it at the glass. We heard it crack, we heard a piece break free, and we heard it fall. We winced for the clatter as it hit the stone floor, but there was only the softest of taps, and then silence.

Hazel's hand was slim enough to get through the jagged gap. The key turned and the door swung open.

Within the conservatory, dimly visible, there were chairs and tables, and climbing plants covered the back wall of the house. Set deep within the ivy the French doors did not yield. We peered through the glass. The faintest of light from under an inner door showed a wall covered in bookshelves but nothing more. We could not be sure there was a key in the lock.

It was Hazel who tried the solid back door to the house. It moved when she turned the handle. We pushed it, and yellow light spilled out. There was a distant murmur of voices, but we had not disturbed them. We opened the door further and were looking into the heart of the house. A wide corridor with arched alcoves on either side stretched away in front of us, and the light came from the far end where the corridor opened into the hall. We stepped inside. In the recess of each alcove there was a door, and it was from the furthest of these that the voices seemed to come.

We closed the door behind us to hide our entry, and moved step by step deeper into the house. The light came from a single globe and it was dim, but if anyone stepped through any of the doors, we were on display. We had to hear what the voices were saying, and we were halfway along the corridor's length when the voices suddenly became louder as the far door opened. We turned to run. The back door was too far to reach. In a panic we pressed ourselves into the nearest alcove.

"I shall regard this evening as the beginning of the Christmas festivities." It was Oscar, overflowing with bonhomie, heaping praises on everyone and everything in sight, and literary enough to work semi-colons into his speech. "A meal to remember, my dear lady; a truly magnificent repast – and the company –" his voice wheezed into a purple patch – "the company inexpressibly delightful."

He was so confident that for an instant we thought we had made a mistake. He was in no danger. Then we glanced at each other, and remembered the skewered eye.

A woman laughed. It was a seductive sound, and I knew it. "And there is more celebration to come, Oscar," she said, "if you have the stamina."

"Dear lady, don't tempt me."

"Allow me to show you the library," said Beatrice Cole, "and see what awaits you."

Hazel turned the door handle behind us and we stepped through. We had nowhere else to go. We were surrounded by books, barely visible. The French windows were our only hope. We felt our way towards them. Long curtains reached the ground. We parted them. The conservatory was on the other side and the dark garden beyond. I touched the handle and felt for a key. It was there. I turned it and pushed. The French windows were old and iron framed. They jerked and jammed. Feverishly I pushed again. They shuddered and creaked open. We were through and pushing them closed when light streamed in from the corridor and the iron frame jammed again. There was a gap from top to bottom, just too narrow for even Hazel to get her fingers through to straighten the curtains we had disturbed.

Beatrice Cole and Oscar Bullimore were silhouetted in the doorway.

"It feels a little chilly in here for you, my dear; allow me to fetch your wrap."

But Beatrice Cole had stepped ahead of him and switched on a table lamp. She wore evening dress and her shoulders were bare. "I think I shall be warm enough, Oscar," she said.

"I thought perhaps a window was open." His small round glasses glinted against his ruby cheeks as he glanced round the library. He was about to betray us. We shrank down until the room was out of sight.

"Oscar." There was a tinge of impatience in Beatrice Cole's voice. "Forget about me and think of yourself and what you mean to us."

He was glad to oblige. He chuckled. She had driven all thought of an open window out of his mind. We heard the clink of glasses and the sound of liquid. Without breathing we moved closer to the uneven chink in the curtain. Oscar was sitting in a high-backed armchair at one end of the library table, Beatrice Cole was opposite us pouring brandy from a decanter into glasses, and just coming through the doorway was Mr Slade.

He was in charge. There could be no doubt of that. His long, sallow face with the high forehead regarded the room calmly. He seemed taller than I remembered. And he was handsome despite the mesh of scars. His hair was black, and his features were solemn. He was a man to trust.

"Come in, Mr Slade, and sit down." Oscar seemed to be playing the host, and I saw why when Slade began to come forward. He moved very slowly as if every step caused him pain. He held one arm stiffly at his side, but it was his face that reflected what he felt. His mouth twisted from time to time, disturbing his scars and making it necessary for him to dab his watering eyes. The constable and the pale girl flanked him, ready to give support if he should stumble. It was the girl who pulled out a chair at the opposite end of the table to Oscar, and he sat down.

There was a drawn-out silence caused by nothing more than Slade taking infinite care with his stiff arm, supporting it with his other hand until it was resting on the table while everyone in the room watched. When he cleared his throat before he spoke he tilted his head as if even this caused him discomfort. "Mr Bullimore." The voice seemed to have no relation to his mouth, which was small and pink-lipped. It came with a liquid rumble as if something boiled deep within his chest. "I propose a toast to your great achievement."

Beatrice Cole and the constable raised their glasses with him, but the thin girl remained behind

Slade's chair, no more than an attendant. "To Oscar Bullimore," said Beatrice Cole, "our Founder."

"Our Founder!" they repeated, and drank.

Oscar, bathing in their flattery, beamed at them, but was nevertheless slightly puzzled. "Founder?" he said. "Good heaven's above, what do you mean? Founder of what?"

Slade put down his glass. The constable left his side and went to stand behind Oscar's chair. Oscar smiled up at him. Beatrice Cole leant across the table. "Surely you remember us, Oscar," she said. "The night of the rats?"

18

Oscar Bullimore got to his feet. "Thank you for your hospitality, Mr Slade, but I think the evening is drawing to a close." He was puffing out his moustache in an attempt to sound jolly, but the constable's hand fell on his shoulder and he collapsed back into his seat.

Slade raised a hand. "Just before you leave us, Mr Bullimore, we have something to show you." The liquid rumble in his throat had increased to such an extent that his words were distorted and he turned away to take a napkin that the pale girl had ready for him. He buried the lower part of his face in it and worked away at his mouth while he cleared his throat. It was an action that anyone would want to perform in private, but Beatrice

Cole and the constable greedily absorbed every detail.

When he eventually lifted his head, his small lips were pinker than before and the napkin he let fall was bloody. "Miss Cole," he said, "would you kindly introduce our new guest." There was still the sound of fat frying in his throat but his voice had become peculiarly divided and echoed within the library.

Beatrice Cole stepped out of the circle of direct light that the lamp shed on the table and went to a curtained alcove at one side of the fireplace. She paused before she pulled back the curtain, glanced back over her bare shoulder with all the seductiveness she had once directed at me, and said, "Let me show you something else you will remember, Oscar."

There was a rattle of curtain rings and light from the room penetrated the alcove. We heard a shuddering gasp from Oscar, but we, in the darkness outside, were as motionless as spiders.

Within the shadows of the alcove loomed the gigantic figure of a man. No features were visible in his face, his arms were close to his sides, and his legs were together. He was a huge man, standing at attention, and at the sight of him, Hazel's fingers dug into my arm so fiercely that I turned towards her. The man-shape was the rusty colour of baked clay, and we each knew what it was. The terracotta coffin.

Slade's guttural rumble seemed to coat

everything in the room. "Yes, Mr Bullimore," he said. "It is what you think it is. It was fashioned by the Marquis de Terre Cuite himself, and we brought it here."

"You stole it." Oscar was able to sound contemptuous.

"We have it by right. We alone are true to the Black Dawn which was founded by the divine Marquis. His work continues."

"Absurd!" Oscar was defiant. "I wish to see no more."

"It will entertain you." Slade nodded briefly to the girl at his side. She crossed the room to Beatrice Cole and together they swung back the coffin's lid. What it contained remained hidden in darkness, but between them they manoeuvred a wheelchair up to it while Slade's voice continued.

"The recuperative properties of this casket are remarkable," he said. "I myself have rested within it, when need be. It helps bind foreign tissues together, and while we have been dining it has been assisting our friend here."

The two women turned away from the sarcophagus and brought the wheelchair, and what it contained, to the table. Jeremy sat there. In this light Oscar could hardly be aware that he was sitting opposite a corpse, for Jeremy was half turned away so that the devastation of his face was not visible. Nevertheless Oscar was alarmed.

160

"What's this? What's going on?" It was bluster, and no one replied.

Slade got to his feet, turned his back, and slowly began to make his way to the door with the girl in attendance. "I will leave you to converse for a moment," he said, and the door closed behind him.

There was silence in the room. Hazel knew that there was worse to come, but nothing could prepare her for how bad it would be. I put my arm around her waist and held her tight as Oscar twisted to look, first at the constable behind him, and then at Beatrice Cole. They did not say a word. It was Jeremy who spoke.

"Welcome to our circle, Mr Bullimore," he said. There was a spasmodic twitch to his face but no more, and only by an effort could I recognize the slur and slither of his nightmare voice. "Without you, Mr Bullimore, we would never have come together. You, more than anyone, are a true member of the Black Dawn."

"No!" The voice alone had been enough to repel Oscar. "No – I refuse to join you!"

"But you must." The corpse heaved up a raw, raking laugh. "You and I, Oscar Bullimore, are brothers under the skin!" And Beatrice Cole swung Jeremy around so that his full face was towards Oscar.

There was a tiny sound from Hazel, a kitten's whimper, but within the room it went unheard. I

161

crushed her to me to prevent either of us moving. On the far side of the table Jeremy and Beatrice Cole were side by side, and both were grinning. Jeremy's grin was caused by the exposed teeth on one side of his face; her grin was wide as she devoured every detail of Oscar's expression.

The stillness hung from second to second until, slowly and clumsily, the corpse tilted slightly and Jeremy's arm, which had been out of sight, came into view. He displayed his flayed wrist and hand. The sinews showed, and the fingers painfully opened and closed under the lamp. "Remember the rats, Mr Bullimore," said the naked teeth.

Slade had returned. He stood in the doorway. "So you see, Mr Bullimore, everything you wrote about has come to pass." With his attendant he came to the table and sat himself down. He took up the napkin, reached to his mouth and peeled skin from his tongue. "Not to everyone's taste, Mr Bullimore," he said, "but a rather striking example of the art which you…" he paused, lifted his hand and pointed at Oscar's chair and, as he did so, the corpse also lifted its hand and pointed "… a fine example of the art which you, Oscar Bullimore, did so much to restore."

Oscar was dumb. His face was mottled. His eyes were fixed on Jeremy as Slade extended his fingers and the flayed hand did the same. Then with his other hand Slade began tugging at his fingers as if taking off a glove. The skin came away. It was an extra layer of skin, an elbow-length glove, and as it peeled away so Jeremy's stripped fingers became limp.

Slade laid the skin glove on the napkin. "Miracles do not come without cost. It is a relief to stand aside for a while." He pointed to the napkin and spoke to the girl at his side. "Put this where it will come to no harm."

She hesitated as if afraid to move, but then timidly stooped forward and murmured something to him.

"The eye?" There was a trace of impatience in him but he turned to Oscar with a smile. "Our friend who sits so quietly before you, Mr Bullimore, is a man of many parts, as you may have noticed." His smile widened a fraction. "But one of those parts is missing. He lacks an eye. It may interest you to learn that it is outside, keeping watch. I see what it sees." He pointed at his own right eye. It had a red rim. "I have borrowed a portion. The discomfort you see is the price I must pay, but removing what I have borrowed is a delicate task and will take up too much time. We have work to do."

"Work?" Oscar had found his voice. It was hoarse and feeble. "You need do no more. I am convinced."

Slade got to his feet. "Look at me, Mr Bullimore," he said. "What you see in me is a man who can never be overcome. I died in the midst of a crowded market place, but I sucked life from another … and I am here!"

Oscar was breathing hard as he struggled to bring back his courage. He could only mutter, "I would need proof of that."

Slade, seeing no danger in Oscar, became conversational. "You have a young friend who could have assisted you to understand. He saw me within Death's shadow, yet I was able to suck new life from a mere fragment of flesh – a finger from an arm severed only that day from a patient in hospital and discarded by the surgeon."

Now I knew that it was a freshly amputated arm that had lain beneath him in the market place, and I had seen the girl cut off a finger and hold it to his lips.

"The finger was mislaid in the stress of the moment." Slade seemed amused. "My assistant, however, was able to recover it using processes known only to members of the Black Dawn."

I had caught a glimpse of the girl as Hazel and I saw the finger squirm. Now the girl stood at his side as he turned stiffly towards her as if to pay her a compliment. The movement, however, had in it the threat of punishment and she, like a frightened child, held herself rigid and gazed at her feet.

"Even she," said Slade, "can exercise power at a distance. But I go further." He leant forward deliberately to allow the light to oil the pallid blotches of his face. "I alone have taken the final steps in the rituals of the Black Dawn. I am remade in my own image, and shall never end. I shall devour the world!"

Oscar stirred as if he would get to his feet, but the constable's hand was heavy, and Slade said, "Please remain where you are. We shall have need of you … eventually."

He made a gesture dismissing the girl, and no one spoke as she gathered the napkin containing the skin-glove and the skin from his tongue and turned away. It was as she moved that my mind unlocked. "Stay here." I breathed the words to Hazel, stepped back from the window and moved stealthily towards the door into the house. I was racing the girl, and a half-second before she came out of the library I had eased the door open a slit and saw her step into the corridor. She crossed to a room opposite and as she went in bright light flooded from it. I had seen what I needed.

I crept back to Hazel and drew her away from the window. With our heads close together I whispered, "When the girl gets back come with me."

Hazel's fingernails bit into my hand as if we were exchanging strengths. We watched. Beatrice Cole placed a case of polished wood on the table and opened it. We saw a glint of metal inside. "Your instruments, doctor," she said and handed him something from the box.

"Doctor may be something of a courtesy title, Mr Bullimore," he said, "but since we began our experiments with hospital parts I have acquired some surgical experience, as you can see." He pointed a scalpel at the body in the chair. "A living subject is preferable. However, I am afraid our dear departed friend here slipped from us before our procedures were completed. One of us was a shade too enthusiastic." He glanced at the constable who tilted his expressionless slab of a face as if acknowledging a compliment, and bore down on Oscar's shoulder to prevent him moving.

"But tonight our founder has joined our company in order to assist us." His voice was the grating of pebbles in a watery undertow. "Mr Bullimore will provide abundant fresh tissue to enable us to continue."

"No!" The roar that came from Oscar lifted him from his seat and dragged the constable with him as he lunged across the table at Slade. He did not quite make it and was being dragged back just as the girl returned to the library. It was what I had been waiting for. I tugged at Hazel and drew her away.

The noise of the struggle allowed us to move quickly. In the dim corridor a gleam from beneath the door showed us the room the girl had entered. I pushed back the door and we were blinking in the bright light of a kitchen. My eyes searched feverishly before I found what I expected. Hazel saw it too, the white chest against the far wall.

"That's where they keep everything they've used," I said. "It has to be."

She began to move towards it but there was one more thing we had to do. "The eye outside," I said. "We need that, too."

In the corridor we could hear the struggle continuing and we ran to the front door careless of being overheard. Outside, we knew where to look. Hazel shielded the beam of the flashlight and we approached the eye from the rear. It was held in a fork with only the ragged outer tissue skewered.

"Something soft," I murmured. "He mustn't feel it."

She gave me her handkerchief and I draped it carefully over the eye, gambling that Slade was already distracted by Oscar's struggle and perhaps would think that some night creature lurking in the garden had tilted it so that it was dimmed. I lifted it gently and put it in my pocket.

The disturbance inside the house had settled. There were voices but we could not hear what was said. In the kitchen we went to the freezer and lifted the lid.

It was all there. On top was the napkin and the skin. Below it were what appeared to be joints of meat. Limbs and parts of limbs, recognizable hands and arms, and other parts wrapped in plastic.

There was no horror for me in that moment. I was numb to it. I had worked out my plan and I had no time to think, so as I began pulling the skin, Jeremy's skin, over my own left hand, my mind was filled only with hatred and a passion for revenge. Hazel had twice my courage. Seeing what I was doing, she lifted out an icy arm, unwrapped it and found alongside the flayed skin that belonged to it.

I looked at her once, questioning what she intended. She moved stiffly, almost too rigid to do what she was doing, but she simply shook her head at me and carried on.

The skin had a clammy texture and was cold. My own skin refused to accept it and shrank within it. I saw Hazel wanting to scream at what she was doing, and when her hand was, like mine, gloved in the grey film she forced herself to do what I could not allow myself to do. She clenched her fingers. The arm that lay on the table made the same movement and we both made the same moan of disgust.

The sound of our own voices shocked us to silence. We listened. No footsteps in the corridor. We had not been heard.

"Quick!" It was Hazel who led the way. Even at that moment I wondered how she could steel herself for what she did next. She lifted up the severed arm and took it with her.

We got back to the conservatory. The struggle in the garden room was over. The constable had one arm round Oscar's neck, choking him. Like a nurse, Beatrice Cole was taking instruments from the box and laying them on the table. Slade had got to his feet and was shuffling forward to select one. Between them, Jeremy's corpse lounged in its seat with his flayed hand resting on the table. I wore the skin of that hand. I did not dare curl my fingers.

It was Hazel who had to crouch and tug at the frame of the glass door. It trembled and stuck. I had to keep one arm stiff but I grabbed the edge of the door with my free hand, and we pulled together. The door moved an inch and wedged itself tight. It had to be enough. My mind was running with hers, and when she crouched and pushed the severed arm through the gap and laid it on the floor inside I knew what she intended. She advanced her hand that was gloved in the flayed skin and flexed her fingers. The severed arm did the same. Its raw fingertips dug into the carpet and hooked the arm forward.

Then she looked up. "The eye," she whispered.

I kept my gloved hand steady as I reached into my pocket with the other. The eyeball, wrapped in the handkerchief, was as heavy and soft as wet sand. I lifted it delicately and laid it gently on the ground.

Within the room no one spoke. They were concentrating on Oscar. His head was on the table, held there by the constable's weight, and one arm was stretched out. Beatrice Cole was rolling back

Oscar's sleeve, and Slade was fussing with the instruments while the pallid girl held a surgical dish. We had to rely on Oscar's heavy breathing to cover what we did next.

We watched the severed arm. It dragged itself across the carpet like a huge spider hauling its sack of eggs. It went under the table out of view of everyone in the room. Only we saw it clawing itself closer to the hem of Beatrice Cole's evening dress. It reached and touched. Hazel turned back her wrist and opened her fingers wide. The spider reared its legs, fingered the air and suddenly hooked forward. It held the hem.

I had my heel over the eye as it lay on the flagstones. Within the room there was the desperate hiss of Oscar's breath as he struggled to free himself. The hand tugged at her dress and Beatrice Cole looked down.

Hazel spoke quietly. "Now!" she said.

I sensed the eye under my heel and trod sharply down with my full weight. For an elastic moment it held and then, with a soft explosion, it became an oyster mess.

And Slade screamed. The scalpel he held clattered to the table and he bent double as he backed away with both hands clutching his ravaged eye socket.

The constable tipped Oscar and his chair over backwards, left them sprawling and ran to Slade.

170

We saw Beatrice Cole beginning to turn towards them when she caught sight of what was scuttling up the material of her gown. She was too horrified to scream. She threw up both hands and began to back away as if the red-nailed spider was not already clinging to her. Hazel rose from her crouch with her hand clawing the air, making the fingers crawl spider-like higher and higher up the dress towards uncovered flesh.

My gloved hand was also moving, and Jeremy was moving with me. We reached across the table, Jeremy and me, and we fingered the handle of a scalpel, slid our fingernails beneath it, and grasped it. We had no more movement than our forearm but it was sufficient. We raised it. The constable was leading Slade back to the light, begging him to lift his hands away to reveal his injured eye.

"No, you damned fool!" Slade pushed him back. "Someone has got it. Find him!" In his blindness he lunged at the constable, pushing him towards Jeremy. And Jeremy was waiting.

The constable took a step back, and Jeremy's arm came up. Another step, and Jeremy struck. The blade was slim and sharp. It went in. Jeremy took it out and sliced once, twice and then held it firm, pointing upwards as the wounded constable lost his balance and fell. He impaled himself on the knife and lay back across Jeremy's lap while Jeremy's half-face looked down on him and grinned. It was the last smile the constable ever saw.

My own eyes jerked away to Beatrice Cole. Her white throat was in the grip of a red hand. Even at that moment she seemed to be trying to back away from it as if she was too squeamish to put her own white fingers to the raw sinews that were working the gleaming knuckle-bones. And in the corner of my eye there was Hazel, one hand clasped around the wrist of the other to give it strength while her fingers tightened and tightened until they became a fist and at last Beatrice Cole clutched at what clung to her throat. She was too late. She was choking for breath and it had too strong a grip. She fell. Her hands loosened. We watched a spasm jerk her once, twice, and then she lay still.

And the room was quiet. Suddenly no sound, and no movement. Hazel, horrified at what we had done, was rubbing the last remnants of torn skin from her hand. We were both murderers, and I was seeking more. My eyes darted around the room searching for the one I had to confront. Oscar was stirring but only one person was upright. I saw the tortured face of the girl and I was across the room, in front of her, menacing.

"Where is he?" She shrank away, wedging herself into the corner, bullied and helpless. In that moment I saw myself, standing amid carnage, part of it, glorying in it. I was sickened and stood back. There was no danger in her. She was a slave. But I had to find her master. I asked again, "Where is he?"

She pointed to the door into the corridor but just as suddenly drew back her hand, terrified at having betrayed him.

Oscar was heaving himself to his feet, and Hazel was helping him. I held his elbow. "Slade has gone." I pointed to the door. "I'm going after him."

"No." The choking he had endured still robbed him of breath. "Too dangerous." He pointed to the box of instruments on the table. None of us had seen Slade leave, but he would be armed. I went to the fireplace and picked up a brass poker. I hefted it, but already Oscar had lumbered ahead of me and blocked my way.

"Tell me where they are." He was short of breath. He saw I did not understand and he put a hand to my chest to hold me back. "Where do they keep them?" he gasped. "The limbs … the severed limbs."

I waited. He had something in mind. "Slade –" he drew breath – "he's experimented on himself." Oscar's small eyes probed mine, forcing me to understand. "His face," he said, "all those cuts. He has been replacing himself!"

The girl in the corner was nodding. She was helping us, and it had already dawned on Hazel what Oscar was saying. "You mean some of Slade is with the rest of –" she gestured – "that stuff in the freezer?"

"Where is it?" Oscar was in charge. "Show me."

We went into the corridor, the three of us together. The house was hollow with silence. There was a strip of bright light under the kitchen door. We listened, then burst it open. The kitchen was empty.

It was Oscar who lifted the lid of the freezer. He was only for a moment horrified, and then he made an effort to snort through his moustache in the old style and growled, "Well it's me own fault – who wrote the bloody stuff in the first place? So think, Oscar lad, think!"

Then, with an effort, he plunged his hand among the parts. "What have we here? A nameless portion of anatomy. God-damned useless." He threw it to the floor. "An ear? Not what I'm after." Frozen, it rattled across the tiles. "Give me something large and juicy – something I can get me gnashers into!" He lifted a long parcel. "Aha! This is the boy!" and he peeled the plastic off a complete arm. He pushed up his spectacles and examined it. "Male," he said, "and slightly the worse for wear. Those crooked fingers would never do for a surgeon, do you think? And something I noticed about dear Doctor Death was his very beautiful little hands. What do you think we have here, arm replacement therapy? This is Slade's own arm and, if I'm not mistaken, he's still sensitive to this mising part of his anatomy!"

Oscar, I wanted to say, you're not in the middle of one of your books now, but he turned on me as if he'd heard. "You with the poker, guard the door, will you? While the young lady here will help me light the stove." He saw my mouth open. "I'm not thinkin' of cookin' the damn thing, Donald – get to your post!"

Then he was giving orders to Hazel. "Gas ring will do, me dear." She had found a box of matches. The gas popped on the top of the stove. "Just what the doctor ordered. This'll help smoke him out."

He had opened his mouth to laugh at his own joke, but no sound came. There was a rush of feet in the corridor, a sharp cry, and then silence. Hazel was nearest the open door. I pulled her back and started to go forward.

"No! Don't move!" It was a female voice. The pale girl stood in the doorway. "Please don't move." She stood there with her hands clasped in front of her, and for a full second I thought she had fled from the horrors in the other room ... until I saw that she was not alone. There was a figure at her back, clutching her arm and holding a bright scalpel to her throat.

"*Doctor* Slade, I presume." Even at that moment Oscar could not curb himself, but his theatrics had no effect.

The phlegmy voice rattled at me. "Throw that down!"

The poker clattered to the floor, and the eyes in the blotched but handsome face were now on Oscar. "One false word from you, writer, and the girl joins the rest."

I heard Oscar draw in his breath but before a word escaped his lips the scalpel glinted prettily and a red thread appeared on the girl's neck. It was so slight, so sharp that she did not appear to notice it. It was a warning.

"Now you, Bullimore, put down what you hold." The steel tip touched the girl. "Slowly, Bullimore. One false move and her blood is out."

"This yours, is it?" said Oscar, holding the arm aloft before he laid it across the burning gas.

The cry from Slade's throat was thinner than the arc of the bright scalpel blade as it sliced air away from the girl's neck. The sizzling tendons of the severed arm tortured the tendons that held the knife and jerked it back against the will of Slade.

The girl twisted free, stumbled, crawled into the corridor and Slade, superhumanly against the pain that seared him, twisted also and stooped to strike. Oscar turned the arm on its nest of flame. It hissed, and through the stench of burning flesh Slade screamed again. He jerked his arm but it disobeyed him, made a grotesque circle above his head and the scalpel scored a deep cut across the top of his skull.

We watched him flail. We saw a man whose own arm attacked him. He ducked and weaved, trying to avoid the blows it aimed at him. He backed from it but it was his own arm that drove him and there was no escape. He strove to open his fingers but the shrivelling sinews had locked the bones to the blade and he slashed himself across the chest. Blood welled through his jacket. He reached up to guard himself with his other hand. The blade pierced his palm, pulled out, then drew a line across his brow and began to peel his face. His handsome features were hanging down in tatters when Oscar, in disgust, pulled the arm from the flame. It went skittering across the tiles and lay at Slade's feet, twitching and writhing as he disembowelled himself and fell across it in a rain of parts.

Epilogue

There were inquests. A group of maniacs had murdered an investigative journalist and had threatened a famous horror story writer and two young friends. The group had all died during "satanic rites" that had backfired.

I shall never make a journalist. I rejected all offers to tell my own story. "And you could have made a killing," said Oscar, but he was thankful that I never revealed the existence of the little story, written by himself, which began it all. And he took to Hazel in a big way. "She'd have been the only girl for me," he said. "She can come up to London any time she likes and I'll wine her and dine her until she never wants to leave. You can come too, if you have to." We did, and still do.

The pale girl was never found. "Just as well," said Oscar.

He still writes his novels. "Who else," he says, "supplies happy endings like me?"

Have you read...

FACETAKER

Philip Gross

THE UNTOLD TERROR IS OUT...

The station was a cast iron vault. Look round on ground level and you're in the present, with red plastic signs and automatic glass doors that hiss open with their electronic eyes. Look up, you could be in a burned-out cathedral.

Denzil needed a photo taken, some ID or other, so we walked past after school. This was a couple of months after the Pinkus affair. We'd spent a bit of time together. He didn't have friends exactly, not a group of them. He'd just stride into school from a slightly different direction from everyone else, in that long black coat with lots of buttons, kind of Seventies retro-style. He wasn't unfriendly – certainly not shy. Some days he'd just walk in and sit down, smiling very slightly, tapping his fingers as if he had a Walkman you couldn't see. He'd sit back a bit and watch the rest of us through slightly hooded, sleepy-looking eyes. First time I asked him what he was thinking: "Oh," he said, "just observing." People have tried to say he must have been lonely, left out, but that doesn't make sense to me. If Denzil came in and sat down on his own, you started to feel it was everyone else who was left out. That was the power. I couldn't imagine being like that, not caring what anyone thought of me. I wished I could. After a while I'd drift over to him, and if he felt like it he'd let me in on what he was thinking. With Denzil, that was being friends.

As we entered the station concourse there was a

noise so loud it hurt. On platform one the InterCity was powering up in a haze of blue diesel steam. It started as a whine and it built to a roar, like fifty pneumatic drills in competition. It's a big station, a junction, and half of England seems to change there, passing through. Up among the iron girders, there's a century of smoke and soot, full of echoes and feathers and bird lime and an emptiness that's always there, looking down on our small hurrying lives the way we might look at an ant's nest.

The noise shook loose about a thousand pigeons in a panic. Then the brakes hissed off and the train started slowly, with a noise like metal grinding on a lathe. For a time we couldn't talk or think, so we watched the carriages slip past, getting faster, and there were faces framed in every window, staring out like clothes-shop dummies. Masks; I suppose there were people inside them, but how could you ever know who they might be?

"Damn," said Denzil. "There's somebody in there."

The photo booth was pushed back in the corner of the concourse, between an industrial-sized grey rubbish bin and a pile of rubbish that was meant for it but had missed. From the whitish plastic walls a more-than-life-size woman's face gazed out with blue eyes and butter-blonde hair. The more I looked at her, the more unnerving her too-perfect teeth became. Behind it, the brick wall was the colour of dried blood and ashes. Beneath the hem of the little grey curtain, we could see a bit of raincoat and some feet. That's all I registered at first glance, and Denzil was already passing the time by felt-penning out one of the photo girl's front teeth, so we laughed about that for a bit. It was several minutes before we noticed that the woman in the booth didn't seem to have moved at all.

Two, three minutes, that's all it should take. And Denzil didn't like queuing. The reason he walked everywhere, with that long-legged lope of his, leant slightly forward, was that no way, he said, would he ever stand in line and wait.

"Hey," he said suddenly. "Some legs!" I looked under the curtain and grinned ... then winced. Poking out from the hem of the grubby grey coat were two hugely swollen ankles, wrapped in surgical bandages, round and round. The dressing couldn't have been changed for weeks, it was so mud-stained and fraying. In the creases of it, brownish blood or pus had leaked, then caked and dried.

Alice the Bag. She was a local feature around the station, along with the down-and-out kids with thin whispery voices, in all kinds of accents. They came and went. Then there was VI, the hulking moon-faced one who didn't look like a beggar at first because he wore a jacket and a tie, a different tie each day. "Excuse me, spare a copper for a cup of tea?" was his opening line, or sometimes, "Excuse me, but we've lost our train fare home, me and my brother…" The voice was polite but not quite right, a child's voice in a grown-up body. He was slow. The village idiot, Denzil called him once, VI for short. But Alice was queen of the patch. You saw her trudging slowly, hunchbacked, or stopping to lash a new find to her broken trolley. I'd seen her hundreds of times, but not from this close. You didn't, not if you could help it. She was famous for her smell.

"Yech," I said. "Go in there after *her*, you'll have to burn your clothes when you get home."

I looked again, at those legs. I couldn't help it. The really sick thing was that at their ends, crammed on over the bulging bandages, were carpet slippers, flip-flops with still just a trace of pink fun-fur.

"She's asleep," said Denzil. "The old bat's having a snooze." It was true. Five minutes at least we'd been there, and you could see from the way her knees had lolled apart that she'd slumped back. I was surprised we couldn't hear her snoring.

"Hey," I said, "do you think she needs a passport? Where do you think she's going?" For a horrible moment I imagined her prettying herself up in there for the photo, going coy and girly, fluffing up her thinly frizzed grey hair. I looked at the slot in case a strip of four of her slipped out, glossy and wet, but there was nothing there.

Denzil was pacing. "Come on," he muttered. "I haven't got all day." He gave a loud excuse-me cough. No response.

"You could give her a nudge," I said.

"Huh. After you."

"No thanks."

"OK, so we knock." He banged. It must have been loud in there, an inch or two from where her head must be, through the thin plastic wall. She did not stir.

"Oh, leave her," I said. She was getting a wink of sleep in a dry place; we couldn't really begrudge her that. I didn't like to think where she slept by night, in her carpet slippers.

"No way," said Denzil, not to her. "I want my photos. OK, Mr Nice Guy. You wake her up nicely. How about a morning cup of tea?" And he jerked the little curtain back.

"Excuse me," I said. No reply. I held my breath, leaned in and tugged her sleeve.

It happened slowly, in stages. First her arm slithered off her lap and flopped at her side. As I jumped back, the weight of it overbalanced her and she began to crumple towards me. She wedged in the door for a moment, she was so wide, with her head lolled forward, then it rolled the other way, and she slithered on out, with a soft thump on the pavement. She rolled over halfway and lay, her face up and her feet still twisted at an angle in the booth.

Her mouth lolled open, with a few grey teeth here and there in the gums. Pushed forward in among them, I could see her tongue. Her eyes were open and dull, and for the first time in my life I knew that I was looking at a real person, really dead.